"It's a boy," I hear someone say

A flannel-wrapped bundle is placed on my chest.

Ever so gently I put my arms around our son, feeling his warmth, hearing his first whimper. It's as if there's no one here but my baby and me. I close my eyes, my heart crashing into my ribs as I lie perfectly still and let the feelings roll over me. Feelings of love so intense it takes my breath away, feelings of connectedness. This precious little boy, who lived all these months as part of me, will remain part of me forever.

"Look, his eyes are open," Andrew murmurs, his own eyes wet with tears.

Andrew touches the tiny fingers and I see his hand tremble. "So this is Jonathan. Should we pick a second name for him?"

"Just Jonathan," I whisper, my heart swimming in happiness.

Dear Reader,

After the publication of *Heart of My Heart* in April 2008, I was humbled by the words of praise offered for my first book. Reading reviews by readers and receiving e-mails about how much they enjoyed my book thrilled me, and gave me a feeling of accomplishment that was as exciting as it was appreciated. Having such wonderful feedback has changed my life. Thank you.

I am delighted to offer you my second book for Harlequin Superromance. *Baby in Her Arms* is one woman's story about finding happiness after the loss of her husband. Emily Martin, like so many wives who find themselves alone, turns to her family and friends for support, and finds that love is once again possible.

This story was inspired by my parents' love for each other, and my mother's bravery in facing life without my father. When you read this book, my one wish is that your life will be enriched by Emily's experience as she searches for happiness in her new life.

I would really appreciate your feedback on this story, as I believe *Baby in Her Arms* offers hope for each of us, whatever the future holds. If you can relate to what happens in the life of Emily, Andrew, Zara or other characters in the story, I would love to read your comments. Please contact me at www.stellamaclean.com, or e-mail me at stella@stellamaclean.com.

Sincerely,

Stella MacLean

BABY IN HER ARMS
Stella MacLean

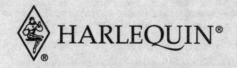

HARLEQUIN®

TORONTO • NEW YORK • LONDON
AMSTERDAM • PARIS • SYDNEY • HAMBURG
STOCKHOLM • ATHENS • TOKYO • MILAN • MADRID
PRAGUE • WARSAW • BUDAPEST • AUCKLAND

Recycling programs
for this product may
not exist in your area.

ISBN-13: 978-0-373-71553-4
ISBN-10:   0-373-71553-6

BABY IN HER ARMS

www.eHarlequin.com

Printed in U.S.A.

ABOUT THE AUTHOR

Stella MacLean has spent her life collecting story ideas, waiting for the day someone would want to read about the characters who have lurked in her heart and mind for so many years. Stella's love of reading and writing began in grade school and has continued to play a major role in her life. A longtime member of Romance Writers of America and a Golden Heart finalist, Stella enjoys the hours she spends tucked away in her office with her Maine coon cat, Emma Jean, and her imaginary friends while writing stories about love, life and happiness.

Books by Stella MacLean

HARLEQUIN SUPERROMANCE
1487–HEART OF MY HEART

Don't miss any of our special offers. Write to us at the following address for information on our newest releases.

Harlequin Reader Service
U.S.: 3010 Walden Ave., P.O. Box 1325, Buffalo, NY 14269
Canadian: P.O. Box 609, Fort Erie, Ont. L2A 5X3

This book is dedicated to all the women who have survived the loss of the one person whose love enriched their lives and fulfilled their dreams.

ACKNOWLEDGMENTS

To Paula Eykelhof, my editor, and Adrienne Macintosh, associate editor, who turned this story idea into reality.

To Deb Hale, a Harlequin Historical author who has never failed to offer advice and encouragement.

To Judy Good, Isaobel MacKinnon and Diane Lockwood, who have supported my efforts in so many ways.

CHAPTER ONE

IN MY HASTE, I NEARLY banged my head on the revolving door as I hurried into the hospital. Just my luck to get stuck in traffic for over an hour on my way here! A precious hour during which my grandson emerged into the world.

When I'd finally made it to the hospital parking lot, I was forced to wedge my fifty-five Ford T-Bird between a pickup truck and a van. I wasn't pleased, the potential for damage to the paint job being very high. Ignoring the likelihood of scratches and bruises to my beloved car, I scurried toward the entrance.

Of course it didn't help matters that I dropped my purse at the elevator doors, scattering the contents, including a stool sample from my cat, Fergus. I had been driving to the vet clinic when I got the call from my overwrought son-in-law, Gregory Cardwell.

Gregory definitely doesn't have a way with words even on a good day, but today was his worst by far. I waited impatiently as he told me that Zara had just made it to the hospital in time. My dearest and only daughter, who'd always lived life in the safe lane, must have been frantic as they rushed through the doors.

"Excuse me. Please excuse me. I need to get on this elevator," I said, eyeing my lipstick and nail file wedged against the chrome leg of a seat positioned next to the elevator doors. Scooping up these articles within reach, including the stool sample, I scrambled onto the elevator, leaving the lipstick and nail file to fend for themselves.

"You dropped this, ma'am," called the security guard as he held up the errant tube of lipstick.

I snatched it from his hand, thanked him and smiled at the other occupants as the elevator doors closed and we rode up to the maternity floor without a stop.

Clutching my grocery list with the room number scribbled on the back, I approached the nursing station. "I'm Emily Martin. I'm here to see Zara Cardwell, room 301."

"Fourth room on the right," the nurse said, and I walked down the corridor. I passed mothers-to-be walking with their tummies proudly displayed, and mothers carrying their newborns, some of them accompanied by men, looking ecstatic or harried or both.

Ah, I'd found the room…. I peered inside. My daughter's dark auburn hair veiled a tiny form cradled to her breast. I stopped and clutched the door for support. All the words of relief and congratulations—words about how lovely she looked and how happy I was—disappeared at the sight of this child of mine who'd taken on the mantle of motherhood right before my eyes.

The light from the window seemed to make the sheets shimmer. The pale blue cap on my grandson's head enhanced the pink glow of his tiny cheeks. Zara's gentle touch and soft smile as she stroked his tiny fingers offered a picture of everything beautiful in this world.

Seeing them together, I remembered another time—when I'd held my newborn son, tears of joy blurring my vision. Somewhere deep inside, I could still hear Andrew's words the first time he held Jonathan. "It doesn't get any better than this, this moment of knowing that someone else shares in who you are," he'd said.

As I stood watching Zara, my heart flooded with love. And I was suddenly aware that my life was about to turn in an entirely different direction. From now on, the baby lying so peacefully in her arms would be the focus of her life.

Would she ever see me the same way again? This daughter who'd been my lifeline, my reason for getting up in the morning these long, lonely months?

"Zara, honey. Sorry I'm late, but I got stuck in traffic. Are you okay?" I moved into the room. Gregory was nowhere in sight, which secretly pleased me. He and I don't really see eye to eye on anything except maybe date and time—*if* he'd look up from his video game designing long enough to glance at the calendar and the clock.

"Mommy, isn't he perfect?" My daughter's teary gaze met mine as she held my grandson out to me. "He just finished nursing, and we were talking to each other about our day. Would you like to hold him?"

Babies talking? I highly doubted it, but I understood the sentiment. "I'd like nothing better," I replied enthusiastically, peeling off my coat and tossing it on the chair.

"Mom, you have to wash your hands first!" Zara said, edging the baby closer to her body to protect her dear one from the unseen menace of germs.

"Good idea," I agreed, remembering my morning and the contents of my purse.

I scrubbed my hands to the elbows, giving my watch a good going over in the process and probably gumming up the works. But what did it matter?

"There, I'm ready." I stuck my arms out. Our eyes met, and something magical passed between us—as if, at some level, we needed to mark this moment, this feeling that she and I were sharing a miracle that only a mother and daughter can experience.

Zara smiled with pride as she handed her son to me. His bundled form rested in my anxious arms. Holding him ever so carefully, I was filled with adoration. His eyes were closed and there was only the occasional movement of his tiny lips. As I studied him, my foolish attempt to slow the tears catching on the rim of my glasses failed utterly.

"He's beautiful. So beautiful," was all I could say as I lowered myself into the armchair by the bed. What I felt as I stared at the baby in my arms made words superfluous. I touched his cheek, the velvety warmth of his skin connecting me to him. Love, like a physical thing, surrounded the two of us as I eased him closer. Time slipped away, and I was back in the moment when I'd first held the most beautiful little girl in the world—his mother. Overwhelmed by a sense of longing so powerful I was unable to move, I closed my eyes, waiting for the feeling to ebb.

"He's so gorgeous," Zara whispered, stroking the back of his head as I held him. "We want to name him after Dad."

My throat tightened with the memories that stubbornly refused to fade. "You do?" I whispered.

"Yes, we're going to call him Andrew Martin Cardwell. What do you think?"

I looked down into his sweet little face. Andrew Martin Cardwell would never know his namesake, never hear his grandfather's voice or be taken for long walks in the woods in springtime. But having Andrew's name would be the best possible way to remind him of who he was and where he came from. "Your father would be so happy to know you named your baby after him."

"And we've done it for you, as well, Mom. Gregory and I want you to be happy. I've said this all before but…" Zara's smile barely disguised the hope in her eyes.

Like a torrent of water from some unseen place, feelings of loss swept over me, clearing a chilled path in their wake. Andrew had been gone over a year, and yet there was never a day when I didn't miss him. And never more than in this moment of celebration.

How did the word *happy* always manage to do this to me? I was happy, for heaven's sake! I had what everyone was so fond of calling "a life."

I just didn't have the life I wanted.

"Zara, darling, don't worry about me. You've got so much to look forward to, especially the happiness this baby boy will bring you. It's you, Gregory and baby Andrew who matter now."

"I feel so differently about everything," Zara said wistfully. "I'm a mother, and I'm going to be the best mother I can. And you showed me how."

Oh, darling daughter, don't do this. Don't reduce your mother to a blithering, mascara-smudged idiot.

I wanted to turn away while I dabbed at the tears once again blurring my vision, but stubbornness and pride made me stay right where I was.

"Mom, please don't cry. You know what I'm saying is true. I wouldn't be nearly so relaxed about all of this if you hadn't talked to me about everything, told me how you managed with us. God, I couldn't imagine delivering two of him." Zara made a face.

"You would've done it if you had to and done it well, the way you do everything in your life."

"Probably. I am my mother's daughter, after all. Are you prepared to take on your grandmotherly duties?"

"Absolutely." Zara didn't know just how much I meant that. My son Jonathan's little girl, Megan, lived in Bellingham, Washington, a long flight from Portland, Maine. Since she'd started talking to me on the phone, we had had lots of chats, but it wasn't the same. I needed to feel her little arms around my neck, bake cookies and dig in the garden with her. I'd bought her a watering can, but she'd been here only once to use it.

"Maybe you'll clean out Dad's office and turn it into a playroom for Andrew when he comes to visit. He'll need lots of space for all the toys you'll buy him," Zara teased.

What a nice way for my daughter to bring up her favorite topic where I'm concerned. My three children had been after me for the past few months to clear out Andrew's office, convert the room to a den or playroom, in order to launch this new life they're convinced I should be leading.

They didn't understand that taking my husband out of the house I'd shared with him for thirty-five years would remove whole chunks of me in the process. Parts I couldn't bear to be without. Memories…like the way Andrew made me feel when he opened a bottle of wine for just the two of us. The smell of the aftershave he'd worn for thirty years, the first bottle being a Christmas present from me. The way he piled pillows behind his head before he did his habitual reading at bedtime.

If I got rid of his things and removed him from my house, I was afraid I might start to forget him. Forget how he looked when he frowned in concentration, or how he smiled for no real reason. I couldn't let that happen. He needed me to keep his memory alive.

My love for Andrew had been a driving force in my life. There was never a day when the sight of him didn't thrill me. When he walked into the kitchen in the morning and hugged me, my day brightened. We loved mornings, the urgent confusion of children leaving for school, followed by a few minutes alone together before Andrew left for work. Our lives were hectic, special…and in the past. As I thought about it, I didn't really need his office to keep memories alive for me, but I did need my daughter to be happy. "If it'll help you concentrate on your son, I'll clean out the office. But it'll have to wait until you children take what you want from his framed prints and his coin collection."

"Mom, your little ruse isn't going to work. Jonathan and Connor and I talked this over. We want you to put all of Dad's memorabilia in boxes and we'll go through them when Jonathan and Connor come home at Christmas. No more excuses," she whispered, reaching to take my grandson from my arms. "You have plans for your grandmother, don't you, Andrew?"

It was the gentle tone of her voice, the near reverence in her words as she cradled Andrew that threatened my emotional calm. I felt the old familiar tears and told them to back off. Baby Andrew's life was just beginning, and my daughter needed to be free of her worry over me.

"Zara, I promise to get started on your father's office the first spare minute I have, but for now, I'm going home to phone everyone about my grandson."

"That's great, Mom. I haven't had time to call anyone yet. I can't wait to tell Jonathan and Connor."

The fact that my grown children were close friends gave me such pleasure. Although Connor and Zara were fraternal twins and very close to each other, they always included their older brother, Jonathan, in their lives. Zara and Jonathan were the two who tended to look at a situation from all angles before they leaped, while Connor, my wild child, jumped first and asked questions later. "Your brothers will be so pleased to hear from you, and to know that Andrew's arrived safe and sound."

"And Mom, we'll never forget Dad. How could we? But I want my mother to find herself."

"I'm lost?"

Zara chuckled. "Of course not. You've simply spent your life making our lives special—Dad's and ours. It's time you discovered what makes *your* life special."

"Don't the things I do for my children qualify?" I gave her a raised-eyebrows smile and patted her playfully on the head. Deep inside, I wondered exactly when my daughter's voice had taken on that mother-knows-best quality.

I DELIVERED FERGUS'S stool sample before going home. Of course, the traffic behaved itself and I found myself pulling into my driveway before I realized it. My house, with its massive brick facade, its matching brick chimneys at either end, its tall, elegant windows, was my dream house. Since I'd been raised in a tiny bungalow in a subdivision where every house looked like every other one, 1345 Postmaster Lane was home, the perfect house.

There was only one tiny flaw. The very kind, but very peculiar person who lived next door. Sam Bannister, with his bushy eyebrows, towering frame and penchant for reading Shakespeare out loud in his back garden during the summer, often seemed to be lurking somewhere on his property.

Oddly enough, Andrew and Sam had been good friends, and my husband had not made friends easily.

But what really unglued me was that ever since Andrew's death, this scion of the university community had taken it upon himself to keep tabs on my comings and goings. Of course, he had the perfect opportunity when he mowed the lawn, a task he'd taken on when Andrew was sick. Maybe that was what retired classics professors did with their free time. I had no idea. There were days I got up and left the house way earlier than I needed to, simply to escape his prying eyes.

Now, like a thief in the night, I eased my bulky car along the driveway toward the garage as quietly as I could, trusting fate to let me park and escape into the house before Sam poked his head over the hedge.

I should've known better than to trust fate because there he was, doing his usual giraffe pose as I walked out of the garage. *Okay, be nice...* "Good morning, Sam. Lovely day, isn't it?"

"It is at that. The woman on the Weather Channel says we can expect this to be a typical autumn day. How are you doing?" he asked, eyes burrowed deep under his bushy eyebrows, his whiskey-colored hair with shots of gray at the temples peeking out from under the straw hat he wore.

"I'm fine. In fact, I'm better than fine. Zara had a baby boy this morning. I just came from the hospital."

He did that funny little skip of his and appeared from behind the hedge. "That's wonderful, Emily. You must be pleased. What's his name?"

"They're calling him Andrew Martin, after his grandfather."

Sam smiled. "Your husband would be so happy." He paused. "I remember when the twins were born."

What? "You do?"

"Yes, you two had only been living in the house a few months, I believe. And my dear Evelyn had died the spring before that…. Yes, I remember it well."

Sam Bannister having fond memories? Who would've believed it? Certainly not me. He always seemed to be living in another world…possibly another galaxy. "Yes, Andrew would've been very happy to be a grandfather again."

"Grandchildren are great, aren't they?"

"Yes, they are. How's Phillip?"

Sam seemed to shrink a little at the mention of his grandson. "He's doing quite well. He's nearly seven now, and quite a handful."

Sam had one child—a son, Robert, who hadn't visited his father very often until after Phillip was born. Lots of reasons for that, money being the first that popped into my mind.

Stop being so cynical and enjoy the day, baby Andrew's birth day.

"I'm glad to hear your grandson's doing well." I searched my mind for something else to say but came up empty. "I've got to get going and make a few phone calls, tell everyone about my new grandson."

He nodded. "You do that, and we'll catch up later. I have some ideas I want to discuss with you about this hedge. It's dying. I'm considering replacing it with a fence."

Sam Bannister may have some peculiar qualities, but he could make anything grow. "Well, if you can't save the hedge, no one can. And a fence sounds like a good idea."

"Fine. Then we'll have tea tomorrow afternoon to talk about it."

Tea? In the afternoon? When had Sam decided to be so friendly? And why did it matter? This was a day of new beginnings, and a cup of tea was a small price to pay to improve our adjoining properties. "Okay. See you tomorrow."

I turned away and made a beeline for the back door, shoved the key in the lock and ducked inside.

Fergus was waiting in the window of the breakfast nook when I got to the kitchen, his fur all plumped up and a look of complete disdain in his eyes. "Don't give me any trouble," I warned him. "Thanks to you and your bowels, I'm the laughingstock of the hospital," I said, stroking his huge tail vigorously.

Fergus is a Maine coon cat who rules my life with

an iron paw. But the unvarnished truth is that he'd become my best companion since Andrew died. He always seemed to understand when I needed him to leap up on the bed in the middle of the night…when I couldn't sleep because of all the thoughts crowding my mind. And the regrets tugging at my heart.

"Fergus, I have to call Kate with my news. So no howling while I'm on the phone, promise?" Fergus had this really annoying habit of breaking into cat song at about the same time as Kate picked up the phone.

I dialed Kate's number and she answered on the first ring.

"You have a grandchild, right?" Kate said.

"Yes, a grandson, and his name's Andrew Martin Cardwell."

"After his grandfather. How wonderful. Emily, you must be delighted." Kate's voice was filled with warmth and caring that never failed to bring me to tears.

"I…I am." I wished Fergus would let out with a howl so Kate couldn't hear my voice thicken.

"This calls for a celebration. I have a caramel coffee cake in the oven and I'll be over as soon as it's ready. How's that sound?"

"Fantastic. I have a few other phone calls to make."

I raced to finish my calls. So much more fun than the bathroom I'd planned to clean.

Still, the all-seeing goddess of housecleaning would have her sacrifice this morning, because of what I'd promised my daughter. I imagined Andrew's office looming at the end of the hall, waiting for me to enter.

I felt the old familiar pang of regret, this time over wondering what today would've been like if Andrew had been here to share it.

To ease these feelings, I told myself that if Sam Bannister could change his tune, I could clean a drawer in the few minutes before Kate came roaring into the driveway.

Sitting bolt upright in Andrew's office chair, I ignored Fergus's entreaties for a place on my lap and opened the bottom right-hand drawer.

I'd never in my life gone through anything in my husband's office, so I didn't know what to expect—except maybe a bunch of files and possibly some reference texts. Or maybe a dried-up box of chocolates. Andrew had been an incurable chocoholic all his life.

No box of chocolates. Not even a crumpled candy bar wrapper.

Instead, I found…letters? And beautiful vellum stationery?

Never in his life had Andrew ever written anything to me on paper like this. Pushing Fergus's furry face away, I pulled out the drawer, releasing it from its track, and hefted it onto the top of the desk.

Had I discovered his private letters…love letters? Oh no, this couldn't be what I thought…but why else would he be using such beautiful paper?

Unable to breathe past the lump pressing against my throat, I took out the first letter. The house seemed to be holding its breath as I stared at the envelope suspended between my fingers. A letter meant for someone else…

Anxiety made my limbs go weak. No, it couldn't be. Not here in this house, our house. And what if I knew her? My fingers twitched to tear the beautiful envelopes into tiny fragments and hurl them into the fireplace.

But if I didn't open them, I'd never know what they contained, who they were meant for and why. Gingerly, I took the rest of the letters out of the drawer and spread them on the desk. There were eleven—I could still count over the pounding of my heart—and they all appeared the same.

No name or address on any of them, simply a number printed in Andrew's narrow script on the upper right-hand corner of the envelope.

I closed my eyes and tore open the first one.

CHAPTER TWO

Dearest Emily,
It's November 20, and I'm writing this letter after seeing Dr. MacKinnon this morning. He told me I have a deadly form of lung cancer, and the prognosis is very poor. On the way home in the car, all I could think about was you.

How can I tell you something like this, something that will change everything between us? I love you so much.

You'll never know how badly I wanted to bare my soul to you today, to tell you how terrified I was. I wanted to pour out everything the doctor said, have you comfort me, do all the nice things you always do whenever I am in any kind of trouble.

But then I remembered our conversation over breakfast this morning and all your plans for Christmas. I wanted what was almost certainly our last Christmas together to be perfect, and I knew how much you were looking forward to the holidays. I wanted our time with the children to be one of happiness, not clouded by the ugliness of my disease.

As you are so fond of putting it, "God gave you a poker face and an ability to keep secrets that would've done the CIA proud." I pray you're right.

When I got home from the doctor's office a few hours ago, you were in the kitchen, flour and cookie sheets all over the counters. I needed to bury my face in your neck, feel you laugh against my chest and your arms around me!

I decided then and there that I'd keep a diary of the months ahead, in the form of these letters. This dreaded disease has taken any pretense from my world. There's no time left for anything but complete honesty with myself…and thankfulness that I got to live the life I wanted with the woman who made me feel so special.

When I look back on our life together, I realize that so much of how we loved each other came from our belief that our love could survive anything. What we had together was more about focusing on what was good in our marriage. We learned so much from each other about love and loving. I need to share what I remember best about our life together, about how you loved me, made me feel so positive about myself. But most of all, how lucky I was to have you in my life.

The best place for me to begin is with the day I met you at the university bookstore. You were engrossed in reading a text on early childhood development. I remember watching you as you tucked a strand of hair behind your ear and rubbed the bridge of your nose, making your glasses slide sideways.

Then I spoke to you and you raised your head. The slight frown and the way your eyes widened in surprise was so endearing. The way you looked at me, with your warm scrutiny and gentle smile, scrambled my thoughts to the point that I couldn't think of anything intelligent to say. I had an overwhelming urge to touch you, feel the softness of your hair right there in the middle of the bookstore.

I'd never been good at dating, but meeting you made me determined to try. Our first real date was at the campus café. When you walked in the door and smiled at me, my fate was sealed. We had coffee and chocolate doughnuts while we talked. You listened to every word I said and answered my ideas with your own. In fact, you seemed genuinely interested. I found out later that you were interested in just about everything, which is why so many people loved to talk to you.

After that first date my days were measured in how many hours before I could see you again. Then I nearly blew it a year later when I got cold feet about getting married. The day your father showed up at my dorm and ordered me out to his car, and we set out for the local pub—that was one scary ride. When he plunked a beer down in front of me and wanted to know why I wasn't going to marry his daughter, I nearly flipped out. He told me no man, alive or dead, was going to hurt his daughter without offering an explanation.

He talked and I listened. The more he talked, the more I realized that my fear of getting married had to do with my upbringing and not with you at all.

When we'd first made our wedding plans, I was happy and looking forward to our future together. Then, the weekend I went home to tell Mom and Dad I began to wonder whether I was making the right decision. Back in the house where I grew up, I saw how cold and withdrawn my father was, and how he always equated any display of emotion with weakness.

That's when I began to worry that I was just like my father—a heartless, self-absorbed man who couldn't show love or affection. What if you ended up wishing you'd never married me? I couldn't tell you any of this because I was ashamed of how my father treated my mother.

Thank God, I listened to your dad. I could have lost the love of my life and the man who turned out to be one of my best friends. Steve Madden was the father I wished I could have had. What I wouldn't give to talk to him now.

During our marriage I tended to keep my emotions to myself. I've come to understand how much you wished I would share more of my feelings with you.

And so the letters that follow are my attempt to tell you how I felt about the things that really mattered in our lives. These letters are going to be about you and me, about what you've meant to me.
Love always,
Andrew

LONELINESS AND NEED for the man I loved rushed through me, taking my breath. How well I remembered our first date. The way his eyes seemed bluer when he smiled. His laughter at my inept attempts to be funny. And those agonizing moments when we got back to my dorm and I was so sure he'd kiss me. He didn't, and I was convinced I'd never see him again.

To my surprise he asked me out the next weekend, and the weekend after that. I'd learned that Andrew Martin was very good at keeping his cards close to his chest.

But how had he kept his cancer a secret all those horrible weeks? And at Christmastime, with the children there…

I read his letter again. I could see his face that day when he came into the kitchen—the open appreciation in his eyes. My man of few words gave me a hug that nearly crushed me.

When he told me the doctor was running some tests, why didn't I ask what kind? Why didn't I sit him down right then and there and make him tell me everything that had happened during his doctor's visit?

That last Christmas with him was wonderful, one of the best. Jonathan and Linda came home with Megan, who was barely three. I remember Megan's squeals of laughter when her grandfather tickled her.

Because my dad cared enough to talk with Andrew—and my husband was willing to listen—we went through with our marriage plans in the end. But I'll never forget the day Andrew mentioned in his letter—the day he said he wasn't sure we should get married. I was devastated.

I came home to my parents' house and hid out in my room. When I told my parents what had happened, their sympathy only made me feel worse. My two younger brothers, who never tired of teasing me, stayed out of my way. But neither Fred nor Albert could stop staring at me across the dinner table, making me feel like I had a giant *Reject* stamped on my forehead.

Once, I caught a bit of conversation between my parents, in which my father threatened to "beat a little common sense into that head of his." With my father, once the idea was put into words, the actions weren't far behind.

Almost two weeks later, my father came back to the house, a triumphant look on his face. He avoided answering me when I asked him if he'd talked to Andrew, but I'd seen my father on the move before, when one of his children was unhappy.

Soon after, Andrew arrived at the door, to tell me how sorry he was for doubting our love, and I was ecstatic. We decided on a small church ceremony as soon as possible. I'd put my wedding dress away and canceled the caterers, but with the help of Uncle Max… But that's a whole other story.

"Anybody home?" Kate's voice rang through the house.

I folded the letter carefully and slipped it back into its envelope seconds before Kate appeared at the office door. "I'm so glad you've decided to clean out his desk…"

I glanced at Kate and she got this really worried expression on her face.

"What is it, Emily? Why are you crying?"

"Andrew wrote me eleven letters. I found them when I started working on his desk."

"Oh, that must've upset you. Want to talk about it?"

"No, not right now." I put the letters in the drawer and followed Kate to the kitchen.

Kate's stick-with-it quality was part of the reason I loved her so dearly. Led by Kate Morrison, the home owners in our enclave of houses on Postmaster Lane— a quiet street in a suburb of Portland, Maine—never lacked for ideas on how to landscape the green space in the center of the street, never had to find someone to head up neighborhood watch or go before city council to argue against zoning changes.

Kate was an activist in the nicest sense of the word, and she'd spent the past months trying to activate me— so far, without results.

In the kitchen, Kate had the kettle singing. "Thanks for being so kind to me," I said, and meant it.

"You'd do the same for me," Kate replied as she poured boiling water into the teapot.

I would, in a heartbeat. There's nothing I wouldn't do for Kate. "Well, it's been quite a day so far," I said, opening the glassware cupboard and taking out china tea cups.

"I'd say so. How's that wee baby? And how's Zara?"

"They're both fine, and Zara's going to make a wonderful mother."

"She takes after you, so that's not a surprise."

"I don't know about that, but she managed to convince Gregory to turn down another promotion, because it meant they'd have to move to Atlanta."

"He's lucky his company let him stay. And now you'll have little Andrew to spoil."

I hope Zara's reasons for encouraging her husband not to accept that promotion didn't have anything to do with her concern for me.

CHAPTER THREE

MEMORIES OF ALL THE FEAR and anxiety we'd experienced in those months after Andrew finally did tell me he'd been diagnosed with terminal cancer kept me awake last night. Alone in the darkness, I remembered trying to be upbeat and positive when all I wanted to do was cry. The day we told the children took every ounce of courage and determination we could find within ourselves. What frightening days those were! Yet this morning, sitting at his desk with the morning light warming the room, I feel blessed. My husband, who so often guarded his words, had felt the need to put his thoughts on paper for me. And after a sleepless night, I needed to read them.

Dearest Emily,
Christmas is only a week away and I'm so afraid. I've always been able to keep a secret, but the stakes were never this high or this personal.
I feel as if the world has abandoned me. I feel trapped inside my head, the same thoughts playing over and over: the sense that this is so

unfair, that I may die before I can tell you all the things I need to say.

Sometimes when I'm here in my office with the door closed, I imagine what it would be like to go back in time, back when hope and faith in the future were our biggest assets.

Thinking about you reminds me of how much you loved to dance—yet you spent the best years of your life with a man who had neither rhythm nor coordination. If I could change anything, it would be that I wish I'd been the ballroom dancer you so deserved. Sounds silly under the circumstances, doesn't it?

Remember our first apartment? That third-floor walk-up with heating pipes that clanged all winter. But its biggest attraction was that it came fully furnished. Which meant that we got thrift-store rejects and an old four-poster bed that sagged so badly we ended up sleeping almost on top of each other. But I loved that bed with you so close to me, and the two of us wrapped around each other during those cold nights.

And when the morning light slipped past the wooden slats of the blind and lit the dust suspended in the air, I wanted to snuggle even closer. I loved the warmth of you, the instant you'd open your eyes, your sleepy gaze drawing me to you.

And the desire in your eyes when I kissed you. The feel of your arms entwining around my neck as my eager fingers caressed you, making you groan with pleasure as you moved against me....

What wonderful memories! And how self-assured we were back then, before life tested our abilities to cope.

I remember, too, how strong you were when your parents died. I watched you mourn while I couldn't dredge up the words to console you.

You must have wondered what kind of man you married. What loving husband would go to work and leave you? The truth is, I didn't know what else to do, and realizing I could busy my mind and quiet my heart through work made those weeks bearable for me.

It's only now, with fear and loneliness dogging every thought, I realize how utterly lost and alone you must have felt when I went into work, leaving you to face your grief alone.

Living through these past weeks—not being able to talk to you about my fear while needing you to comfort me—has shown me just what an insensitive person I was back then.

If only I could have found the words to ease your loss. I need you to know I would've done anything in the world to help you. Anything.

I am determined to shield you from this horrible reality as long as I possibly can. If I can hold back my fear and keep my desperate secret to myself for a few more days, I'll feel I've made up for some of those long, lonely hours you endured.

After all these years of you putting me first,
you deserve every bit of support I can give you.
Love always,
Andrew.

I clutched the letter to my chest, and it's as if I was holding Andrew...

After many months of going to bed alone, my body ached for his touch, the feel of his skin, his breath hot on my throat. There was never anyone for me but him. He was my first lover, and my last. Although I can't imagine making love to anyone but him, I find myself envying my married friends. Do they understand how fortunate they are to have someone to love, and someone who loves them and shares their life? How I miss the companionship, the closeness of sharing all those small moments that add up to a life between two people committed to each other.

How well I remember our old apartment. We had so much fun in that god-awful bed. The sex was so new, so exciting. It was Andrew who taught me how to make love.

And, despite his claims to the contrary, it was Andrew who consoled me when my parents died. His arms around me in the night shielded me from the fear that I'd never be able to take a breath without the crushing pain of loss.

I spread the letter out on his desk, aware that the last person to touch these pages was Andrew, my heart clinging to his words.

Unable to bear the tightness in my chest any longer, I decided to go to the kitchen. On the way I passed the living room and peeked in. The old stereo unit we'd bought—our first extravagance—sat in the corner of the room. Funny how neither of us could part with that old thing, despite the chips and bruises that had been doled out by our three children.

And funnier still that he should mention dancing. I loved to dance and I cherished our huge collection of old LPs. The music of the forties and fifties, especially the Tommy Dorsey band, reminded me of the happy times I shared with Dad and Mom.

I moved to the mahogany cabinet and couldn't resist running my fingers over its polished top. Lifting the lid, I turned the knob to start the turntable and listened as the opening notes of Tommy Dorsey's "Stardust" flooded the room.

I moved the coffee table and danced to my heart's content, letting the music lead me through the moves I'd invented those long-ago nights when Andrew worked late.

I was having a great time until the phone rang. As I walked to the kitchen, I looked out the dining room window and saw Sam watering the rhododendrons at the corner of his front porch, the sight of him reminding me that he and I were getting together this afternoon to discuss the fence. The phone call was from Kate, about our shopping trip. When I hung up, I stood there peering out the window at Sam. He was working furiously, his head bobbing in and out of view as he vigorously trimmed away the browned branches.

To keep busy while I waited for Kate, I decided to thaw a few slices of Kate's banana bread from the freezer. It wasn't that I felt hungry as much as I needed to be doing something. Of course, there was always housework, but it was such a lovely day, I thought as I continued to watch Sam in the garden.

Despite his rather awkward movements, I could see by the slight smile on his weathered features that he was enjoying himself. Andrew had often remarked that Sam and I should give gardening lessons, or better still, join forces to start a community beautification project.

Not likely. Sam and I might both enjoy gardening, but that was the extent of our shared interests.

AFTER THE SHOPPING TRIP, during which I spent far too much money on layette items for baby Andrew, I crossed the backyard to Sam's to talk about the fence. As I reached the patio, Sam held the back door open for me. "How was your day?" he asked.

"It was great, and yours?"

"Lots of weeding, a trip to the grocery store. That's about all," he said.

As I glanced down the hall leading to the front door, I noticed the parquet flooring had been replaced with bright blue carpet. I hadn't been inside the Bannister house for years—most of my contact with Sam had been when he'd come to sit on the back porch with Andrew. As I followed Sam into the kitchen, I was pleasantly surprised to see how inviting it seemed with its shiny blue pottery on the ledge above the windows that faced the patio. The house as I remembered it had been bleak, somewhat forbidding. I noticed a large array of photos of his grandson, Phillip, along the bright yellow wall behind the table.

"He's a handsome little boy," I said, pointing to what looked like the most recent photo.

Sam moved around the kitchen island and busied himself making tea before he answered. "Phillip is a dear little fellow, but he's not reading very well."

"Some children read later than others, especially boys. Boys tend to be better at activities that require motor skills rather than reading or writing."

Oh, how dreary, Emily. I sound just like I did when I was a teacher.

Sam approached the table with a tray holding a pot of tea and what looked like homemade muffins. He removed the tea bags while I cautiously buttered a muffin. Not knowing what to expect, I bit into the buttered half and was pleasantly surprised. The muffin tasted like bran with orange and raisin, and literally melted in my mouth.

"This is delicious, just delicious," I said. Eating slowly and tasting the flavors on my tongue, I had to admit that Sam had a talent for baking. But the biggest surprise of all was that for the first time in months, I was hungry.

"It's a recipe I developed a few years ago. I was tired of the standard bran muffin, and wanted something more interesting." He shrugged and gave me a lopsided grin. "Not very interesting, but for what it's worth I like muffins made with buttermilk."

A budding Bobby Crocker? "Do you share your recipes?"

"I haven't yet. No one's asked."

He came to sit down by me and poured us each a cup of tea. I couldn't help noticing his hands. Usually they were covered in gardening gloves, but now as I gazed at them, I saw that his fingers were long, smooth, like a piano player's.

"About my grandson… I'm aware that, as you said, boys learn differently from girls, but I'm still concerned about Phillip. I've been trying to encourage Robert to get him assessed. My grandson may have a learning problem. You don't know the number of children I've seen in the university system whose reading skills were deplorable. I don't want my grandson to end up like that."

There was genuine concern in his eyes, and it made me blurt out, "My goodness, no. When Zara's home and feeling up to it, do you want me to ask her about arranging an assessment? As a teacher, she'd be able to recommend highly qualified people."

"That would be wonderful," he said, his voice appreciative. As he continued to look at me, his features softened with a smile that lit up his blue eyes.

I wasn't accustomed to men watching me this way. After all, at my stage in life, men were mostly utilitarian—plumbers and electricians—or my friends' husbands. The approving attention of a man made me uncomfortable. Yet, I could grow to like this new Sam. He was open, friendly and I felt…feminine.

The sound of a buzzer on the stove broke the moment, and Sam jumped up to shut it off.

"I had to learn to cook or starve, and now I'm quite good at it, if I do say so myself," he said as he opened the oven and slid a pan filled with lasagna onto the center rack.

"I haven't cooked in so long, but I might make a chocolate cake for Andrew's homecoming." My words surprised me, but why not do something to celebrate?

"I'm sure little Andrew will enjoy it," he said, setting the timer.

"I mean, I don't mean Andrew. I—" *Why am I so flustered?*

He peeked over his shoulder at me, a mischievous grin on his face. "I'm teasing, but I'm pleased you've decided to bake a cake."

Is he really? Why?

He placed a pot to soak in the sink and returned to sit across from me.

"So, about the hedge," I said, feeling a little out of my depth and anxious to get to the hospital so I could see Zara and the baby again.

"As I said the other day, we should replace the hedge with a fence."

"As long as it's attractive and easy to care for…" I shrugged.

"We could get an estimate for a cedar or redwood fence."

I'd always assumed Andrew would be here to take care of things like this, and so I'd never really worried about hedges, fences or driveways, which was part of the reason why my children believed I couldn't live here alone. I couldn't have Sam or my children think I wasn't decisive, so in a weak attempt to prove my savvy, I clasped my hands in a businesslike manner. "I agree completely."

"Glad to hear it. Let's have another cup of tea to celebrate our joint venture," he said as he poured and passed my cup back to me. "Emily, I hope you don't think I'm being nosy, but how are you doing?"

Oh dear. Not another person who thinks I need to get a life. "Thanks for asking, but I'm doing very well."

"Are you?" His skeptical glance forced me to look away.

Don't tell me he planned to talk about seeing my lights on late at night. "This past year and a half has been hard, but it's getting much better."

He nodded slowly. "I remember those months after Evelyn died. I nearly went crazy with loneliness. If it hadn't been for your husband, I might have. And of course, I had Robert to raise and that kept me busy."

There would have been lots of women in his circle of friends at the university. If he was so lonely, why hadn't he remarried? Why had Sam chosen to raise a child alone?

And how was it that this man, who'd never confided anything in me, was telling me things now—things that obviously still caused him pain? "I'm glad Andrew could help you," I said quietly.

"He did, and having him as a friend was one of the great blessings in my life. He was such a kind person in every sense of the word. I miss him."

I pressed my lips together to ward off the sudden rush of memories. I recalled those long evenings when Sam and Andrew sat on the back porch and talked about religion, politics and whatever else made the headlines of the *New York Times*. "You and he had some great chats, didn't you?"

"Yes, and I'll never forget him. But that's not what I want to say to you."

Half-afraid of what would come next, I sat back in my chair.

"After my wife died, I used every excuse in the book not to put my life back together. I had my work, my son and my memories. I didn't want anything to change the tidy little cocoon I'd made for myself. I didn't let anyone in, and my life worked just fine— for a while." He paused. "But once Robert left home I had no one."

His expression, so filled with remorse, made me sorry for him. "But you had your work," I offered, trying to make him feel better.

"That's not what I'm talking about. Not at all."

"Then what do you mean?"

"As your neighbor and—if I may say so—friend, I

see you over there by yourself a lot. I'm afraid you spend too much time alone, Emily."

"Sam, that's hardly your business," I said, distressed that he'd been watching me like that.

"Look, I'm probably overstepping the line here, and I'm not suggesting you forget Andrew. From my own experience I know you never will. I'm simply urging you to find someone to make new memories with, or you'll end up alone like me."

He spoke with kindness, offering me a glimpse of why he and Andrew had been such good friends. They shared the same approach to life when it came to telling the truth. And my heart knew the truth of his words. "But you're not alone. You have friends and family," I argued.

"I'm alone in the part of my life where it really counts. I have no one special to spend my days with…because I couldn't—"

"I'm sorry you've had such a difficult time," I said, wanting to end the conversation without hurting this man who believed he was being helpful.

He touched my wrist, his fingers resting ever so gently on my skin. A warm sensation ran up my arm.

"Don't make the same mistake I did. I let life pass me by because I was living in the past. But as of now, I'm making a conscious effort to change my attitude."

"And you believe I should as well?" I asked, feeling cornered by his words.

"I want to be happy again, and you…" He shifted uncomfortably in his chair, easing his fingers away, although his gaze never left mine. "Andrew was worried about you, about how you'd cope when he was gone. He wanted you to be happy."

He didn't have to bring Andrew into the conversation, not like this. I refused to feel guilty about how I chose to live my life by a man I hardly knew, who, by his own admission, hadn't done such a great job himself. "How do you know what Andrew wanted?"

"What do you think we talked about those last few evenings on your porch?"

Part of me resented the fact that my husband would confide in Sam. Petty, maybe even childish, but I wanted Andrew to confide his worries in me first.

It was time to go before I said something I'd regret. "I'll be fine." I got up from the chair and headed toward the door. "I'll wait to hear from you about the fence."

With that I strolled as nonchalantly as I could across the lawn, around the hedge and into the safety of my kitchen.

AN HOUR LATER, clutching a grocery list of what I needed for the chocolate cake, I left. I drove out of the driveway and over to the hospital without bothering to check if Sam was in his yard.

When I arrived at the hospital I went straight to Zara's room, my arms weighed down with shopping bags. She was standing by the window when I walked in.

"Hi, Mom, what's all this?" she asked, smiling in anticipation as she took the bags from me and placed them on the table by the bed.

"See for yourself," I said, delighted with the smile on my daughter's face.

"Mom, you must've spent a fortune," Zara said as she proceeded to open the gifts I'd brought.

"Does it matter? Besides, Andrew needed a few things."

"A few things? There must be a dozen sleepers." Zara lifted out a bunting bag in blue with Winnie the Pooh embroidered along the neckline and down the zipper. "Oh, this is so cute, and perfect for him this winter. And look at all the little shirts and the sweater set with matching cap. Mom, what did you do? Buy out the stores?"

"I had fun. This is the new me, a shopaholic," I teased.

"I'm so glad you are." Zara kissed my cheek.

As I hugged her tightly, long-ago memories washed over me. Memories of the day I brought her home from the hospital, tucking her precious body close as I climbed the steps to the house. Andrew carried Connor, a fierce look of pride and unbridled joy on his face.

But most of all I remembered that instant on the back step, with each of us holding a baby, each in awe of what life had given us. And oh, Andrew's smile that day…

Wishing I didn't have to let go of Zara, I asked her a question. "How are you feeling?"

She pulled away. "I'm getting out later this afternoon, after the doctor's visit. Isn't that great?"

"It is. And you'll be able to rest better in your own bed."

"I hope so. Andrew and I were up three times last night." She glanced over at the bassinet in the corner of the room and smiled wistfully. "And look at him now. He's sleeping like an angel."

Don't get me wrong, I adore my new grandson, but I couldn't take my eyes off this wonderful creature sitting on the side of her hospital bed, cheeks flushed and happiness radiating from every pore. My daughter. "Did you talk to Connor and Jonathan?"

"Yeah, and they're both thrilled. They're coming home for Christmas. Only three months from now, Mom. We'll have lots of fun getting ready for the holidays this year, won't we?"

I spent last Christmas as an emotional zombie while my family tiptoed around me. But it would be different this year. *I* would be different. "We'll have a lovely Christmas. I might even do the cooking."

"Oh, Mom, that would be wonderful. You don't know how much I missed your chestnut dressing last year. The turkey wasn't the same when I cooked it."

My daughter's praise made me smile with pleasure. "And I've decided to bake a chocolate cake to celebrate Andrew's homecoming."

"Chocolate cake? Fantastic!" She hugged me so tight I could hardly breathe and I hugged her back, happier than I'd been in months.

"I'm getting the ingredients this afternoon."

"This is great—hearing you talk about doing things

the way you always used to. Did something happen? Or did my message get through?"

"Both. I started cleaning out your father's office and I discovered eleven letters he wrote to me after he found out about his cancer."

Tears welled up in Zara's eyes, making my heart hurt in my chest. "He wrote to you? My dad, who never ever wrote anything more personal than his name on a birthday card? Oh, Mom, how sweet of him. Have you read them?"

"Two, so far, and I plan to read one a day until I've finished them."

"How can you resist reading them all at once—or are they too upsetting?"

"No, not really," I lied. What else could I say? I wasn't going to make her feel unhappy, especially not today.

"And your anniversary's coming soon, isn't it?" Zara's expression went from tender to worried.

"Don't give it a thought. I'm not." But I did. Constantly. I thought about all the moments lost to us in the past year and a half, all the times I needed Andrew with me.

Baby Andrew cried out from the bassinet in the corner, and Zara got off the bed and went to him. "Here, my darling angel, it's okay. Mommy's here," she said in a soothing voice as she checked her son for a wet diaper and proceeded to change him.

"So, you're coming over this evening after I get home? Do you want to make the cake at my house?"

What I really wanted was to go to my daughter and

tell her how much I loved her, needed her and lived in fear that I'd smother her with all my desperate good intentions. To escape the feelings of helplessness and loss that inhabited my life.

"That's a great idea. I could bake and then do any housework you need done while you rest."

Zara gathered her infant son in her arms and kissed his forehead as she glanced at me. "I know that look in your eyes. You're mentally reorganizing my closet, counting the number of windows that should be cleaned. But I don't want you doing my housework. I want you to enjoy your grandson."

"But I need to feel useful, and you need your rest after the past few days."

"I'll rest, but in the meantime, I'd like you to sit down in that chair over there and hold your grandson."

Nearly yanking the little guy from his mother's arms, I cuddled him as I settled into the chair. "So, are you ready to go home when Gregory gets here, or do you need help packing up?" I asked, touching Andrew's soft, tiny fingers poking out of the blanket. How I loved the feel of an infant in my arms, his soft form, his baby scent.

"I'm all ready," Zara said, tidying her bed table.

"What a perfect time for you and Gregory. Your life will change in so many marvelous ways."

"Sometimes I wonder if I can handle being a mother," Zara said, uncertainty shimmering in her eyes.

Where was that coming from? "You're going to be a fantastic mother, just you wait and see," I reassured her.

"I hope so."

"And your father's office will make a great playroom. We'll have hours of fun with baby Andrew there. I'm going all out with the redecorating," I said, enthusiasm rising in me.

"Yeah, I'm half-afraid I'll come over to find a pony tethered to the lamppost," she teased, the old, confident Zara back again.

Andrew playing in his grandfather's office seemed so right to me. Thinking of my husband reminded me of Sam's dilemma. "I promised I'd ask you for the name of someone to assess Sam Bannister's grandson for possible speech and reading problems."

"Sam? The same Sam who's only ever talked to you about gardening? What's up?"

"Nothing. He's been mowing the lawn for me since your father got sick. Now he's looking into a fence to replace the hedge. He's been very kind and I want to return the favor."

"Don't tell me that man's putting the moves on you. Mom, he's not your type. Besides, there are lots of widowers around, men who do something other than gardening. What about traveling? You often said you wanted to travel. In all the years we lived next door to Sam Bannister, I don't remember him ever taking a trip. He's a stay-at-home, Mom. It's time you had a little fun in your life."

"I'm not marrying the man, I'm trying to find someone to improve his grandson's learning abilities, for heaven's sake," I said, half indignant, half laughing.

Yet I had to admit that Sam's sudden decision to confide in me about his grandson was puzzling.

Zara's focus went from the sleeping infant in my arms to my face. "I'll see what I can do, but in the meantime, *you* could help."

"Me? What good would I be?"

"You were a teacher. You could work with him on his reading. Why not?"

My daughter had a point.

And as I drove home, I went over what she'd said. Sam Bannister might not be my kind of person, but what would it hurt to work with his grandson? That is, if I got the opportunity. Sam or his son might not want my assistance.

But if being helpful to Sam got Zara and the boys off my case, what better proof that I'd gotten a life than to be back working as a teacher for a while?

CHAPTER FOUR

LAST EVENING AT ZARA'S, we toasted wee Andrew's homecoming and I cried a little, but they were happy tears. Connor and Jonathan had sent a huge bouquet of yellow roses, Zara's favorite. The cake turned out perfectly, much to my delight. Zara and Gregory dived into it as if they hadn't seen dessert in months. Pleasing them made me feel so good. I'd held Andrew every chance I had, and this morning I could still smell the faint scent of baby.

With the pleasant memories to offer comfort, I picked up letter number three and opened it, only to find the paper wrinkled, some of the words smudged.

Dearest Emily,
It's January 2, one of the coldest on record, and my hands are shaking so badly I can hardly hold the pen. I've never cried like this in my life.

It's two o'clock in the morning, and I've come down to the office, relieved that you finally fell asleep. If I could've faced this without hurting you, if I could've kept this secret, I would have—anything to save you from the pain

I saw in your face as I told you what was happening to me.

As I spilled my story, you began to sob. I struggled to hold it together as I stumbled over my words of explanation. Telling you about the cancer, how few months I had left to live, was too much, too fast, but it seemed that once I started, I couldn't stop. All the pent-up anguish and fear, the need to share with you what was going on, forced the words out of me. I've never needed you as much as I did tonight.

Sitting here looking at your photo on my desk calms me a bit. I've got to stop this, stop thinking about all of this or I'll go crazy. I want to concentrate on happier times, on those moments when we believed the world was ours.

Remember the day we learned you were pregnant? We left the doctor's office that day, and you insisted that we go and buy our baby a teddy bear. We laughed, made plans and ate pizza, sitting in a street café with our new purchase; his glass eyes staring at us from across the table. And you were so beautiful when you were expecting Jonathan. Did I ever tell you that? I think I did, but if I didn't, or if you've forgotten…you were gorgeous. Your skin glowed and your hair was never shinier. The sight of you on that old sofa in our apartment, a faraway look in your eyes as you rested your hands on your big tummy, filled me with joy.

We'd waited so long for Jonathan, and as soon as he gave his first howl we were hooked on him. I remember how you held him so lovingly in your arms, your expression blissful. Remember how he held his little fists against his cheeks when he cried?

You were able to calm him, while I seemed to make him cry harder. I remember how you used to hum lullabies to him, which surprised me as I believed babies liked their parents to sing songs to them. You were so comfortable with the whole baby business, which made me feel even more anxious about my baby-care skills.

One of the scariest instances of my child-rearing ineptitude was the day you packed him into the carriage and sent me off for a walk in the park. I hadn't gone to the park in years, and was surprised to see so many families and dogs along the meager pathways. The sun on my face made me sleepy, so I found a bench in a quiet corner and sat down.

Obviously, Jonathan wasn't happy about staying in one place, because he started to scream. I jiggled the carriage and made soothing sounds at him. Still he screamed. Embarrassed by the attention of people walking by, I loosened the blankets and picked him up.

I held him facing me and tried to reason with him—to the complete delight of an older woman who strolled by with her dog. Jonathan picked that precise moment to give a kick, which caught me in the stomach and nearly propelled him out of my arms. Terrified of how close I'd come to dropping him, my arms trembled as I clutched him tightly. When we got back to the house, I didn't mention the incident, too proud to admit my clumsiness.

Somehow he survived my failings. I recall the day he toddled around our house for the first time and plunked himself down on the kitchen floor with a big smile on his face. Those times were among the best—learning to be parents, finding out who we really were, what we valued. The three of us were making a life together.

And as much as I love the twins, that first experience of holding Jonathan was life altering. Writing about him has made me feel a little better, but there's still something I need to say, then I'll leave it for now.

No matter what the days and months ahead hold for us, I promise you we will face it together. You've shown me that I'm not alone in this any more. Your love gives me the strength to face whatever comes.

As my grandmother was fond of saying, every cloud has a silver lining. You're my silver lining. Love always,
Andrew

I closed my eyes against the sting of grief remembering those terrible hours when Andrew had explained his diagnosis and what it meant. My husband was dying. So many dreams came crashing down as he spoke the words that completely changed our lives.

My world withering, I listened to what he'd been living through and my remorse knew no bounds.

Yet, for all our pain and grief, Andrew and I were never closer than in those days after he'd told me his awful news. We were trapped in the fight of our lives, a fight we couldn't win. But in those dark times, we found solace in the feeling that there were no barriers between us. We lived for each other.

I grew accustomed to waking up in the night, and from the way Andrew was breathing, I'd know he was awake….

"Are you okay? I ask in the darkness one night.

"Yes." His sigh fills the silence.

"What are you thinking about?" I ask.

"About the time my uncle Jack and I went trout-fishing on the Penobscot River."

"Your uncle taught you to fish when you were young," I say to encourage him while I imagined him as a boy with his fishing rod and tackle—a cute kid with his copper-red hair and freckled cheeks. I wish I'd known him then. I wish we'd gone to high school together. I wish I could've been part of his life from the beginning.

"Hmm… I was around ten, maybe a little older.

Uncle Jack loved to fish. One day we were out on the river in a canoe, and Uncle Jack got a bite on his line, a big fish. He stood up to reel the trout in and in his excitement tipped the boat. He went over the side, fishing hat and all, his line tangled in the stern of the boat…the trout gone."

"What did you do?"

"I braced my hands on the gunnels trying to keep the boat from flipping while my uncle swore and cursed…and laughed. I laughed, too."

My eyes now adjusted to the dim light of the bedroom, I touch his cheek. A muscle jumps in his jaw. "Want to go fishing? We could take off and go up on the Penobscot, spend a few days. I'll watch you fish."

"You'd be willing to do that? You don't like fishing."

"I love fishing."

Andrew takes my hand in his. "And I love that you're willing to lie for me."

"It's up to you," I say, my mind pleading with my heart to hold back the rush of feelings that will drown us both. I want to savor this moment, hold it close and never let go of the intimacy flowing between us.

I rubbed the rumpled pages, feeling the stain of his tears on the vellum, and reread his words. His memories of Jonathan's first few months tighten my throat. And that crazy night I went into labor…

"Hurry!" I yell, flapping my hands over my huge tummy as a sharp pain has me grabbing the bedpost for support.

"You're in labor?" Andrew asks, jumping up from the bed, his eyes wide with excitement as he helps me into my oversize pants and top.

"Get the car started," I say through gritted teeth as another contraction comes. I've got a death grip on the bedpost for this one.

"I'm not leaving you," he tells me, stroking my shoulders as I breathe through the pain.

"They're coming fast. We've got to get to the hospital," I say, meeting his sleep-deprived stare.

"Here, take my hand. You'll need help down the stairs." Andrew hugs me. I hug him back before I waddle toward the door. He's following with my overnight bag.

"I'll be glad to drop this hippo gait," I joke, feeling the beginning twinges of yet another contraction.

"Did I mention I love hippos?"

"Don't flirt with me. I'm in agony," I moan.

"Got it."

Andrew gets me into the car, and by the time I groan through another contraction we're at the emergency entrance of the hospital. Andrew is all business as he helps me into a wheelchair and up to the delivery room.

I grunt and complain my way through the next contraction. I'm about to scream with the pain when my stretcher is wheeled into a room with a huge light hanging from the ceiling and aimed at my nether regions. My feet are stuck in stirrups and there I lie, feeling like a trussed-up turkey.

I clutch the cotton gown barely covering my body and gaze up into Andrew's anxious face. "Don't look," I warn, seeing his strange pallor.

"I love you," he whispers, his hand clasping mine.

"Love you, too." Another contraction glows red-hot across my consciousness.

"Push!" someone yells.

I push, pant and scream, all the while holding on to Andrew's hand.

Suddenly the pain stops. The room is silent. Then a baby cries. People are congratulating us.

"It's a boy," I hear someone say. A flannel-wrapped bundle is placed on my chest.

Ever so gently, I put my arms around our son, feeling his warmth, hearing his first whimper. It's as if there's no one here but my baby and me. I close my eyes, my heart crashing into my ribs as I lie perfectly still and let the feelings roll over me. Feelings of love so intense it takes my breath away, feelings of connectedness. This precious little boy, who lived all these months as part of me, will remain part of me forever.

"Look, his eyes are open," Andrew murmurs, his own eyes wet with tears.

I ease back the blanket. "So they are."

"Has he got all his fingers and toes?"

"Let's check," I whisper, peeling back the blanket

to have a closer look. His little body is encased in a white shirt and a tiny cloth diaper. I turn the plastic band on his ankle to be sure I have *our* baby, then count his toes.

"Yep, he's ours and he's all here." Andrew touches the tiny fingers and I see his hand tremble. "So this is Jonathan. Should we pick a second name for him?"

"Just Jonathan," I whisper, my heart swimming in happiness.

MY LIFE CHANGED FOREVER that day. Jonathan's needs, his feedings and diaper changes absorbed my life. With Andrew focusing his energies on his law career, Jonathan became my constant companion. We went everywhere together, what fun we had.

The old baby carriage—a thrift-store purchase that, with a whole lot of tugging and twisting would eventually convert to a stroller—meant freedom for me. That beat-up stroller had more miles on it than plenty of cars.

Those day trips to the library were visits with old friends. Dr. Seuss and Beatrix Potter stories were among Jonathan's favorites. While he played and amused the staff, I picked up books to read for myself. The staff loved Jonathan's solemn approach to books, his quick smile. They gave him treats, which he devoured noisily.

How I cherished those times with Jonathan. There were days I worried that I might end up talking baby talk long after he'd gone to school.

Back then, in the early seventies, there were few day cares, and we never considered taking our child to coffee at a friend's house as a playdate. Coffee with a friend was a short reprieve from all the hours of caring for your child alone; any advantage to the child and his socialization skills was incidental.

With Andrew's busy career as a litigation lawyer, working many evenings and often weekends, Jonathan and I had nearly seven years to ourselves before the twins arrived. My aunt Celia always said that Jonathan was older than his age. She was probably right. Jonathan grew up living and playing with adults—until that fateful first day of school.

I'll never forget the morning he entered grade one. I'd stayed awake all night, telling myself it was because I wanted to have him up and ready bright and early.

The truth was entirely different. I was terrified that I wouldn't be able to let go of him when we got to the schoolhouse steps. And I was convinced I'd end up crying all the way home, even if I did manage to successfully deposit him at the school. And if he cried and wouldn't let go of my hand… I needn't have worried. When we neared the building, Jonathan spotted a little friend from his library days. Before I could hug him goodbye, he raced off.

And as the other children grew up, it was Jonathan I depended on. Jonathan never came home from school without checking in with me, and I relied on his responsible nature more than I should have. Not that the twins weren't helpful, it was just that Jonathan and I had a history of being best friends.

Everything about Jonathan was familiar to me, including the kind of woman he married. Linda was a pharmacist, another very responsible person, one who took life seriously. With her long brown hair knotted at her neck, she was pretty in an old-fashioned way, and she loved Jonathan.

There were days, especially in the months after Andrew died, when I wished Jonathan lived closer to me.

Suddenly, feeling lonely, I called his number. His phone in Bellingham rang a long time before he answered.

"Mom, is that you?"

He sounded sleepy, or maybe sick. "Yes, Jonathan. Are you all right?"

"I'm fine. What's going on with you?"

I was convinced that the older he got, the more his voice was like his father's. "You'll be pleased to know I'm going through some of your father's papers in the office, and I'm getting organized to renovate this room."

I heard Linda's voice somewhere behind him, asking who was on the phone. She seemed irritated, but maybe I was reading more into it than was there.

"I'm glad to hear that, Mom."

"And you'll all be home for Christmas, the three of you."

"Yeah, we will."

What was this strange tone in my son's voice? "I can't wait to see you."

"Me, too," Jonathan said, and I heard him yawn. Then it dawned on me.

"Jonathan, it's only a little past five o'clock in Bellingham. I woke you, didn't I?"

"Yeah," he sighed. I could see him so well, the way his eyes would close, just before he winced in embarrassment for me. Or the way he ducked his head when something made him laugh.

"How could I not have remembered the time change?"

"It's okay, Mom. I was going to call you today, but you beat me to it. I've been wondering how you're doing."

As sweet as his concern was, hearing the anxiety in his voice bothered me. Jonathan had a very demanding job as an architect for a national construction company.

"Put your worry beads away. I'm doing just fine."

There was a long pause. "I'm so pleased to hear you sounding upbeat."

"I am upbeat, and looking forward to Christmas," I said, hoping I'd put his mind at ease. Oh, how I missed Jonathan. What I wouldn't give to reach through the phone and hug him. "You'll see how well I'm doing when you and Linda and Megan come here. I'm already working on plans for the holidays."

"That's great. We're excited about Christmas, too."

Was there a poor phone connection or did Jonathan's voice lack enthusiasm?

"Mom, I'm in Boston on business next Friday, and

I'm going to drive up and see you—and the latest addition to the family. Don't tell Zara. It'll be our surprise."

I was thrilled at the expectation of seeing my oldest son. It wasn't until he said he was coming to visit that I realized how desperately I missed his easy manner and quiet thoughtfulness. He was so much like his father. "You read my mind, didn't you?"

He laughed. "Not really. Megan and Linda are spending the weekend in Seattle shopping and visiting one of her classmates from her pharmacy program."

Talking to Jonathan, anticipating his visit this weekend, made my throat hurt with longing for those faraway days when Jonathan would surprise us by arriving home from university on a Friday night to stay for the weekend. Oh, how much Andrew and I enjoyed those visits. "I'll be ready for you whenever you get here. I'll get in a supply of popcorn and we'll watch an old movie."

"You bet. I'm Andrew's godfather, did you know?"

"Yeah, Zara told me last night when I was over there. By the way, I made a chocolate cake for Andrew's homecoming."

"What I wouldn't give for a piece of your chocolate cake, Mom."

"Another chocolate cake coming right up." My oldest would be home to see me…and my chocolate cake.

"Mom, I need to talk to you." Jonathan's voice dropped to barely a whisper.

He'd mentioned starting his own architectural firm. Maybe he wanted to run his ideas past me, the way he often had with his father. "Sure, we'll have a nice long chat when you get here."

I waited to hear more, but he said nothing, which told me something was seriously wrong in his life. I wanted to jump in with a dozen nosy questions, but Jonathan wouldn't appreciate such an intrusion into his personal life. "You know you can talk to me about anything."

"I know, Mom, and I appreciate that."

The anxiety now evident in his voice made my heart pound. "Then it's settled. We have a date. I'll dust off my roaster and cook a chicken. To go with the chocolate cake."

"You do that. See you Friday. Love you, Mom."

"Love you, too."

How I wish Andrew was here. He'd be so happy to find out Jonathan was coming for a visit. Andrew loved to have the children home on the weekends, or anytime for that matter.

He and Jonathan enjoyed going fishing together. I can still see the two of them unloading the old Jeep we had years ago, their sunburned faces wreathed in smiles as they dragged their gear out of the back.

Thinking of Andrew made me wonder how he'd react to my tea date with Sam. And the fence. I could almost hear Andrew's throaty chuckle when I explained how determined Sam was to install one.

Would this desire to talk to Andrew, to tell him how

I feel, what was going on in my life, eventually ease? Would I ever be spared the urge to compare my past with the reality of my present?

CHAPTER FIVE

THE NEXT MORNING, sitting in the breakfast nook with a nearly cold half cup of coffee, I stared out at the flower bed of forsythia and my coveted petunias.

My recurring dream of Andrew calling out to me awakened me earlier than usual this morning. Maybe it was because of last night when I wished I could talk to him. Zara had called to ask if she could bring Andrew over while she went to the breast-feeding clinic today. I immediately agreed. Seeing little Andrew would make a great beginning to my day.

She wasn't going to get here for another couple of hours, which meant I had time to read another of Andrew's letters. Last night as I started to fall asleep, it came to me that reading his words gave me a sense of being connected to him in a way I couldn't have imagined possible. And this morning I woke feeling hopeful I *would* find a new life, whatever that turned out to be.

I couldn't explain the reason I believed this, and a part of me didn't really care why. The important thing was that I hadn't been able to move in this direction until I'd begun reading Andrew's letters.

Maybe this feeling of hopefulness wouldn't last, but then again, maybe it would….

Carrying my coffee cup, I settled into Andrew's office chair and pulled out the next letter. As I tore open the envelope, I noted that it seemed thicker than the others.

Dearest Emily,

What a way to spend the month of February! I despise the experimental treatments I started today, not just because no one expects it to change the course of the disease, but because it makes me feel ill.

I can't begin to tell you how hard it was to go through the treatment with you sitting beside me, wishing me healthy with that defenseless look in your eyes. A look I'd seldom seen on your face before, as you never failed to put up a fight, no matter what the issue.

I love that quality in you, that warrior-woman thing you do so well, your never-give-up attitude. Over the days and weeks we've been learning to cope with my illness, I've seen you struggle to remain hopeful, to deny the reality bearing down on us. And I'm terrified. If you lose hope, I'll die sooner. I have this idea in my mind that your hope is keeping me alive. So you can imagine my fear and sense of defeat when I watched you this morning.

I feel your need for hope like a physical force, and there's nothing I can do to keep your hope alive but take part in this clinical trial…for your sake as well as mine.

When I saw that taking these treatments allowed you to believe in the future, it gave me a reason to go through with it. If I can do anything to ease your anxiety or delay the inevitable loss of hope, I will.

Now, sitting here in my office, gazing out at the rain as it washes over the window, I'm reminded of those early years of our marriage. Being a young lawyer in the sixties and seventies was a heady experience. When I joined Cooper and Edison, I had a criminal trial that garnered me the accolades and attention of the law community in Portland. Other lawyers sought my advice. I was in demand, and I loved it. I was successful even by my father's standards. My professional life was on a roll and I wanted to use my new success to help not only those who could afford my legal services, but those who couldn't. Those pro bono cases made a real difference in people's lives, and I gained so much satisfaction from doing it.

When we bought this house, I could see our future spread out before us. A future of opportunity and privilege. I was so wrapped up in achieving the dream, I never stopped to consider that the life I'd bought and paid for came with another price. In the early years, I could never have imagined letting go of my passion for de-

fending those less fortunate. But I did. At first I blamed it on the workload generated by my paying clients, but that wasn't the truth. I let the lifestyle I'd become accustomed to dictate my professional life...with serious repercussions in our personal life, as well. But I don't want to remember all that went wrong in my life; nor do I want to dwell on that clinical trial. All I need right now is you.

I want to open a bottle of Merlot and pour us each a glass. I won't be able to drink much of it, but I need the pleasant routine of having a glass of wine while I watch you at work in the kitchen.

Seeing you making dinner and chatting about the day has held me together mentally and emotionally more often than I care to admit. My heart warms in anticipation of the pleasant hours ahead for us this evening.

I remembered that night. When he came out of his office, I checked him over carefully, looking for signs that the treatment was making him ill. I didn't see any, which says how good my husband was at hiding the effects of his illness from me.

Of course the wine might have affected my ability to notice any change. The first glass went straight to my head—and moved down from there. We made love on the living room sofa...without closing the blinds on the floor-to-ceiling windows. Thankfully, there were no lights on in the house, or the whole neighborhood would've had front row seats at a peep show.

Afterward, we ended up falling off the sofa onto the floor, where we sat laughing like a pair of fools.

My body warmed at the memory of that night and the fun we had…

"Hello? Anybody home?"

Sam? What's he doing here? I jammed Andrew's letter into its envelope and hurried out to the kitchen.

"Oh, there you are," he said, holding a potted coneflower in his hands. "I've come bearing gifts, and before you say no, I should warn you that if you don't take this humble offering, I will bore you to death by reading Shakespeare in your gazebo."

I chuckled at the image of him holding a book and reading to me, his hair askew as he belted out the words.

I'd insisted on having a gazebo built after we moved in. I wanted a lovely, private space in which to read between nursing the twins.

"No one's ever offered to read Shakespeare to me," I said, surprised yet again by Sam's behavior. He hadn't dropped over like this since the day Andrew was too sick to sit on the porch and he'd only stayed long enough to ask if there was anything he could do.

Don't dwell on the past. Enjoy the moment…and the man who made you smile so early in the day.

"Want to come in?"

"Why not?" he said, putting the plant on the floor and making a beeline for the breakfast nook. He folded his long frame into the narrow space and looked at me expectantly.

"Can I get you something?"

"A cup of tea would be perfect."

I put the kettle on to boil. "Zara's coming over with Andrew in a few minutes, and I'm going to babysit."

"Oh, that's lovely. If you don't mind, I'd like to stay and meet your grandson."

"You won't have to wait long. She just pulled into the driveway," I responded, instantly aware of how Zara would interpret Sam's presence in the kitchen. In Zara's mind, I was not to include Sam as part of my plan for a new life. She'd said as much yesterday at the hospital. I suspected that Zara's idea of my new life was one without a man in it, despite her protests to the contrary.

Before I got the door open, she was out of the car, baby carrier in her hands and diaper bag on her shoulder. A moment later, she entered the kitchen.

"Hi, Mom. I'm running late. Hope you don't mind if I just drop Andrew and run. He's been fed and changed, and he should sleep—" Her startled gaze moved from me to Sam. "Hi, Sam."

"Hello, Zara, and congratulations. I see you have a beautiful baby boy."

"Thank you." She shifted her eyes to me.

"Well, I'd better go," Sam said, edging out of his seat.

"No, please don't leave on my account. I can't stay, but I'll be back as soon as I'm finished at the clinic.

See you." She waved and was out the door and into her car before Sam or I could respond.

"That was quick," Sam said, watching her rush out.

That was impolite, I thought, but didn't say anything. Instead, I picked up Andrew in his carrier and put him on the table between us as we sipped our tea in contented silence.

"Does this bring back memories—having a baby in the house, I mean?" Sam asked, putting his teacup down.

"Yeah. There's nothing like it. I love the smell of babies. I remember when Jonathan was born. Talk about nervous!" I smiled. "And the day Andrew made his first attempt at diapering Jonathan."

"You mean those bulky cloth diapers with the big pins that looked more like spears?" Sam asked, his lips curving up in a smile. "I could never figure out why those pins were needed. Tying knots would've been better."

"You're right." I chuckled at the picture of Sam trying to make the old safety pins work. "And the time Andrew tried to hold Jonathan in his arms with no diaper on."

"Hey, that happened to me, too. I don't think I've ever felt that wet."

We laughed together, the sound reminding me how long it had been since I'd felt like this. Sam's hand brushed mine. A fleeting moment of connection, yet I opened my hand in response. Shaken by the sudden need flushing through me, I fixed my attention on the baby.

"Andrew would've been so proud of this little guy," Sam said.

"Yeah, he was so excited when Megan arrived, and if he'd known that Zara would be having a baby—" I swallowed hard, focusing intently on baby Andrew.

The silence between us dragged on until I felt compelled to glance over at Sam. The vulnerability in his eyes, the way he seemed to be searching my mind, was unnerving. Did he see how emotionally exposed I felt right now? And was it remembering Andrew, or having Sam sitting there looking at me in a certain way that was leaving me feeling raw?

"Would you like a piece of banana bread?" I asked, struggling to come up with a safe topic, escaping the intimate look in his eyes.

"No. I'd better be going," he said, shaking his head as if coming out of a trance. "Would you like me to plant the coneflower in your butterfly garden?"

"I'll do it after Andrew goes home."

Sam moved his attention to Andrew. "Enjoy him. He'll be grown before you know it."

As I watched Sam leave, all sorts of feelings surged through me—feelings of yearning…excitement… awareness.

Attraction?

IN MY URGENT NEED to put my jumbled feelings aside, I took Andrew out with me while I dug a much deeper hole than was needed, and plunked the coneflower into it. Thankfully Andrew slept peacefully in the screened-in gazebo next to the flower bed where I worked.

Sweaty and still restless, I sat down on the teakwood bench in the gazebo to cool off and wait for Zara. I loved this outdoor room with its Boston ivy trailing along the walls, its greenery creating a beautiful backdrop for the huge potted geraniums perched on wooden stands, showing off their bright red blossoms. I was quietly soaking in the peacefulness of it all when I heard Andrew whimper.

"You're awake," I whispered, taking him from his carrier and easing him into my arms. I settled against the lattice of the gazebo, breathing in his baby scent as I raised him to my shoulder and began to rub his tiny back. I closed my eyes, letting the feeling of connection flow through me. He snuggled his face into my neck, and I was overcome with the wonder of holding this baby. My daughter's son. My grandson.

So often my mother used to talk about the glory of each and every moment of contact with a baby. How a new baby was living proof that life came full circle. What I wouldn't give to have my mother here with me now. She would've been delighted to hold her great-grandson.

Andrew squirmed and whimpered again. I held him away from me and looked into his face. He opened his eyes and squinted at me. "Hello, sweetie," I murmured as he continued to squint at me and work his tiny fingers into his mouth.

The sound of a car announced Zara's arrival.

Feeling the need to hold my grandson for just another moment, I tucked him close to my body and watched him peer around.

"We're over here," I called softly.

"This is lovely. You're out in the fresh air with my young man," Zara said.

Andrew turned his head toward his mother's voice.

Zara's expression widened into a smile as she strode across the grass and opened the gazebo's screen door. "How did you and Andrew make out?"

"Just great. He has barely moved since you left. How was your appointment?"

"It went really well," she said, sitting next to the lounge chair where I'd placed Andrew's carrier. As she reached to take him in her arms, an expression of complete contentment suffused her face.

"Would you like to stay for lunch?" I asked, curious as to whether she might mention Sam's being at the house when she dropped Andrew off. Maybe she'd been too preoccupied with her own life to realize that Sam and I had been alone together, although that wasn't Zara's style.

"Thanks, Mom, but I should get home before he starts fussing. I need to feed him and have a nap myself." She yawned.

"Call me later?"

"Of course."

After they left, filled with wonderment at life and all it held, I went inside to finish reading Andrew's letter.

This evening will be like so many with you. You'll prove your ability to take the simplest meal and turn it into something special, which you'll do with even greater care and attention because you're worried. And how much I need for you to make my life as normal as possible right now. And I can trust that you will...the way you've done all our married life. You've always put what I needed and what the children needed ahead of you. You have always provided us with the kind of home life that allowed each of us to discover our own potential.

I never said this, but I want you to know how much it meant to me that you were willing to stay home with the children. I was well aware of how much pressure there was on women to go out and get a job, to be part of the feminist movement.

Emily, I want you to promise me something. When this is over, I want you to find someone really special. Someone who loves you, who shares your passions, your zest for life. You deserve every possible moment of happiness, and a life with someone who loves and appreciates you as I have...and will forever.
Love always,
Andrew

Andrew wants me to find someone special?
Did he have Sam in mind?
What did those two *really* talk about during all

those visits on the porch? Could they have conspired to plan my life without telling me? They wouldn't dare! And Sam certainly hadn't shown much interest in me—until the past few days.

No, it wasn't possible.

My thoughts were interrupted by the ringing of the phone.

I reached across the desk to pick it up.

"Who do you hear from more often than me?" Sam asked.

"Is this going to become a habit?" Yet I felt pleased that he'd called. I have to confess that despite our rocky start, Sam was good company, and I was beginning to enjoy our conversations.

"Is that an invitation?"

"Let me get back to you on that," I teased.

"The main reason I called was to tell you that Monica and John Corey over on Leighton Avenue had a break-in last night. I hope you're locking your doors."

"I only lock the doors at night or when I'm away from the house."

"Well, for your own safety, I'd lock them during the day, as well. Kate's already convened a meeting of the local community watch group."

"Kate didn't mention that when I talked to her."

"Probably because she didn't want to worry you. But maybe you and I should consider putting a dusk-to-dawn light at the back of our properties. With the ravine behind us, and all the trees that could hide an intruder, it might be safer."

Sam was looking out for me…again. Sam Bannister was slipping into my life, becoming my friend. It was kind and sweet, all of it a bit unsettling. Yet, I could easily get to like his attention, his caring. "A light at the back of our properties would make sense."

"I'll see what I can do about getting an estimate. So, how was your visit with Andrew?" he asked.

"Perfect." There was an awkward silence.

"I'm going to Zara's later," I told him.

"I have a confession to make," he said abruptly. "I saw you dancing in the living room the other day, and I've seen you dancing there before."

"Are you spying on me?" I responded sharply.

"No! Never. I mean, I do keep an eye on things, but not the way you're implying."

"Did Andrew ask you to?"

"Not…in so many words." I could hear the hesitation in his voice. "Is this a good time to ask for your help?"

"Go ahead." I was trying to imagine what I could do for him, other than getting Phillip's assessment organized.

He took an audible breath. "As part of my campaign to get a social life, I've been trying to learn ballroom dancing. Believe me, it's not easy for someone with my lack of coordination."

"And?" I prompted, intrigued by the mental picture of this man trying to dance.

"I was wondering if you might be interested in taking lessons with me," he said in a rush. "I'd have a much easier time with someone I know, someone who'd understand when I stepped on her feet."

I couldn't help smiling at the image of the two of us stumbling around a dance floor. I might be light on *my* feet, but hardly light enough to escape the damage Sam's big feet would inflict. "Why me?"

"Because you can dance and I know how much you enjoy it. And I believe your skills could come in handy for me. Besides, we could both benefit from a little nightlife."

I would never have imagined Sam Bannister being interested in dancing. But he seemed set on surprising me at every turn these days.

But if I went to dance class with him, would he get the wrong idea? I didn't want anything more than friendship—and maybe the occasional night out—but surely he was aware of that by now.

Besides, would it hurt if I went out and did something I love?

And, after all, my family wanted me to get a life.

"You're on," I said.

"Super! Now that I'm on a roll, I might as well ask you something else."

"What's that?"

"I was wondering if you'd come to dinner some night soon? I'll make a roast of lamb—Andrew always said how much you like lamb. Would you consider letting me cook for you?"

This is getting too cozy. Too fast. "I'm not sure. With the new baby—"

"You don't have to give me your answer now. I'm ready to cook whenever you're ready to eat."

I hung up, thinking how clever of Sam to make dinner an open invitation. If I didn't know the man better, I'd guess he was trying to date me. He'd certainly developed a penchant for popping into my day, playing Mr. Fix-it, and generally making himself indispensable.

And now he was leaving it to *me* to make a dinner date with *him*. The old fox…

CHAPTER SIX

THE OLD SCREENED-IN PORCH gave me a clear view of my flower gardens, where I'd dug for a while earlier this morning, trying to fix my panic planting of yesterday. I'd half expected Sam to appear and ask what I was doing. I didn't want to see him this morning as I didn't feel comfortable around him right now.

Until recently, my feelings where Sam was concerned related only to his connection with Andrew. Yet, after yesterday, and the way he looked at me when we were alone, things between us had changed. I could feel a shift in how he behaved toward me—and therefore, how I behaved toward him.

There was something so private about that moment when he looked at me across Andrew's baby carrier, the way his eyes seemed to take me in as if I were included in some secret world of his.

Yesterday, I felt a warm connection to Sam, and I appreciated that he wanted to include me in his dance plans. Sam's presence in my life was a newfound pleasure, but dancing? Being held by him while the music played…and what if he wanted to kiss me? It had been so long since any man had held or kissed me… Bitter tears welled up in my eyes. I blinked them back. I couldn't give in to the might-have-been scenarios that had plagued me all these months.

That's not to say I was going to act on his invitation for dinner anytime soon. There was simply no way I could ever see myself making a date with Sam or any man.

When I talked to Zara last evening, she still hadn't mentioned Sam's being at the house yesterday.

I didn't tell Kate during our evening call last night, either. I should have, but Kate wouldn't have settled for anything less than all the details, which would've included sharing how I felt about Sam. And if I didn't *know* how I felt about him, how could I tell Kate?

Oh, how glad I was to have another letter to read…

Dearest Emily,

I woke up this morning to the coolness of early March winds. You were sleeping so soundly I couldn't risk waking you, so I got up as quietly as I could. I was on my way downstairs when I felt the need to go into the room we'd done up years ago as a nursery for the twins. The pale morning sun made the room glow, something I don't remember noticing before.

This spring feels colder than last year, but it's probably me. I'm cold all the time.

The room's changed a number of times over the years, yet as I glance around I remember the yellow paint you and I put on the walls, and the

Dr. Seuss characters we pasted above the wainscoting.

I'll never forget the look on your face when Dr. Reeves said he could hear two heartbeats. The drive home from the appointment that day was a once-in-a-lifetime ride. We were both in shock. How would we cope with two babies? Where would we get the money to buy all the baby things we needed—two of everything?

In the backseat, six-year-old Jonathan talked about babies and how he didn't want too many of them. He had a friend in school with twin brothers, and that wasn't a good plan, in Jonathan's opinion.

Didn't we laugh as we listened to him considering the possible disadvantages of being the older brother of twins?

I recall thinking that twins should show some similarities, but Connor and Zara were complete opposites in every way. Connor was always the child who would strike out with a boldness that had us holding our breath, while Zara sat back and studied the situation.

How could I forget the Saturday morning you hurried into the bedroom and told me to get out of bed and come see what the twins were doing.

Somehow, they'd managed to pull their cribs close together and they were throwing stuffed animals back and forth.

In those first years of raising the twins, I

recall that you and I stopped talking at night. For years after I joined the firm, I'd wake up, feeling lonely and stressed by whatever was going on the next day. And, of course, I'd fidget until you woke up, too. You'd turn on the light and lie back in my arms. Your body always fit so easily against mine. I'd talk and you'd listen as we snuggled there. Soon, I'd begin to relax. Sometimes our middle-of-the-night talks led to love-making; other times we slipped off to sleep. Either way, it was the best part of my day.

And yet somewhere during those years after the twins were born, our nightly chats dwindled. I'd get home later, usually after the children were in bed, exhausted after a busy day. I'd be so tired I'd go to bed and sleep straight through the night, waking the next morning and heading back to the office for another long day.

If I had to do it over again, I would never have put those intimate late-night chats in jeopardy. Even more, I regret spending so many hours in the office. You deserved more of me…better from me.

As I write these words, I can hear you outside my office door. I recognize that nervous pacing of yours. You woke up and found me gone from our bed, and went looking for me. Now you're anxious to know if I'm okay, if I've had anything to eat this morning and if I'm ready to go to the Oncology Clinic. Once you're reassured that I'm fine you'll scold a little about how I shouldn't have gotten up alone, how I should've awakened you.

I love the sense of security it gives me to face the day with you at my side.

I'll stop writing for now. Maybe we'll have lunch out, or go to the bookstore, all the simple pleasures that keep me connected to the real world. Our world.

Love always,
Andrew

The hour we spent over coffee that day in the bookstore, his hand holding mine, the way he fussed over me, made me feel treasured. He should've been worried about *his* health, not mine, but somehow this act of unselfishness reassured me that I could relax a little.

As for those late-night chats years ago, I cherished the nights when we'd lie awake in each other's arms. I was so disappointed when Andrew began coming home too late and too tired for us to share how we were feeling. His preoccupation with work created a barrier I couldn't cross. Caring for twin babies left me too exhausted to question what was going on between us. Each buried in our own responsibilities, we went for days without *really* talking. When those nights disappeared from our lives, I didn't have the courage to ask why—at least not in the beginning.

Andrew was a trial lawyer, and I was expected to

provide a certain amount of opportunity for his clients and colleagues to socialize at our house.

I couldn't make small talk to save my soul. Still can't, but it was worse back then. How many times I wanted to just run away from it all…

Many of the wives in Andrew's circle of professional friends were career women, and so many of them seemed to have an endless supply of witty things to say. The parties I had to host were nothing short of stressful.

There was one night in particular….

Andrew smiles encouragingly from the other end of the table.

I've worked for two days—buying the perfect pork loin roast, the Waldorf salad ingredients, the right wine and an endless list of chores—for the sole purpose of proving that I could host a good dinner party in keeping with my husband's elevated status as senior partner.

By the time I've completed my long list, I'm too tired to make soup, the requisite first course, so I go and buy asparagus soup from the local market.

Andrew seems completely at ease with these people, and I suppose he should be. He works with them every day. I glance at Michael Thompson, one of Andrew's partners, and the one person who epitomizes everything I don't like in lawyers—he's an arrogant, opinionated schmoozer.

I wish I could snap my fingers and turn him into

a toad, but it's Michael's turn to be invited to dinner, and I have to be nice if it kills me. I grit my teeth. I'd rather have a rattlesnake at my table. But knowing that I'm doing something for my husband's career is my reason for maintaining a pleasant expression when Michael asks me, yet again, what I do with my time.

I want to say I work in a brothel and see him give his little cough, adjust his tie and glance down the table at Andrew, his eyebrows ever so slightly raised.

But I'm so afraid that I'll embarrass Andrew, I answer as politely as possible. "I'm busy with the twins. The school library needs volunteers, that sort of thing," I offer as I paste yet another smile on my face.

But being who I am—the overeager wife of a very successful lawyer—I look around the table at these people who seem so perfect, and wish I could disappear. Don't know where I want to be, just any place other than here at my table.

I fantasize about Paris, but so far, the longest trip I've taken is to Charleston, South Carolina, to visit a university classmate.

I excuse myself and go to the kitchen to make coffee to have with the dessert I spent four hours preparing this morning. A soufflé that has to be handled very carefully or it'll be a pile of mush by the time I get it to the table.

Giving the kitchen counter and the collection of

crystal port glasses and china dessert plates a once-over, I return to the dining room to hear Michael going on at length about a new associate in the firm. Someone named Jennifer Sargent, who is the daughter of one of the judges, and a cellist.

Michael's behaving as if this Jennifer person is his wife—or his lover. The look on his actual wife's face as she sits and listens to him heap praise on another woman makes me feel sorry for her.

"Andrew, you're doing a great job of bringing Jennifer along as a trial lawyer," Michael goes on.

I see my husband's quick glance in my direction. "Yes, Jennifer's doing really well. She seems to have a gut instinct for the whole trial business, which makes my job easier."

"She's easy on the eyes, too," Michael spreads his wolfish grin around the table.

I slide into my chair and stare down at my plate. I want to say something nasty but know that I never will, despite the bragging tone of serial philanderer Michael Thompson's comments.

As I scan the table, I can see by the expression on the other women's faces that we all share the same opinion of the man.

The conversation drifts off into politics, and I leave the table to concentrate on putting the soufflé in the oven, relieved to be able to escape.

How could I remember that night with such clarity? Clutching the letter, I feel the old rush of resentment.

"Andrew, how did you manage to spend your working hours with Michael? What an idiot! I'd still like to strangle him."

"Mom, are you okay?"

My heart jumped and I turned quickly, dropping the letter on the floor. "Zara! I didn't hear you come in."

Zara placed the baby carrier on the floor and knelt to pick up the letter. "Is this one of Dad's letters?" she asked, a tone of near-reverence in her voice.

"Yeah, I was remembering a dinner party I gave years ago."

"Was it a good memory?" she asked, holding the letter gingerly in her hands.

"In a way," I said, acutely aware that I didn't want Zara to read what her father had written. Reading Andrew's letters offered me a wonderful opportunity to connect with him, learn his thoughts, feel his love. I never expected to have this chance to revisit our life together and I treasured every word. I couldn't share my husband's memories…at least not yet.

"I have so many memories… Dad and me going fishing. How he would bait my hook. One day in grade eleven, I skipped school and went downtown to hang out at the local arcade. Dad was driving back to the office when he spotted me. I was so afraid he'd tell you."

"He didn't."

"Yeah, and I was so grateful. Dad actually played a game of pinball with me before he drove me to school." She sighed and handed the letter back to me.

I saw the worry lines around her eyes, the way she

chewed her lip, a sign she was struggling to remain calm. "You miss your father so much, don't you?" I asked.

"Yes," she sobbed, wrapping her arms around my shoulders as we hugged each other. Wanting to console her, I hugged her tight, feeling my blouse dampen with her tears.

It was the gentle mewling of her son that brought her out of her misery. I watched as she left my arms and knelt beside the baby carrier: the endearing words she uttered to comfort her son as she lifted him from his tiny world were the most beautiful sounds in the universe.

She glanced at me around Andrew's little body, her gaze tentative. She kissed his head as her eyes locked with mine. I smiled and reached my hand out to hers. "Love you," I whispered.

ZARA'S SURPRISE VISIT lasted about an hour. We had iced tea on the porch while she nursed Andrew. After she left, I was contemplating how pleasant my day had been so far when the phone rang. I checked to see who it was— a very familiar number. "Connor, why are you calling this time of day? Are you at work or did they fire you?"

"Wish I could fire myself. Too damned busy here in chilly Denver."

I looked out the window at the bright sunlight and chuckled to myself. "My sympathies. What's going on in your life? Or are you calling simply to charm your mother?"

"Caught in the act, Mom."

I heard the smile in his voice, and my heart rose. My irreverent son had that effect on me. Connor could charm birds out of the trees. "You just missed your sister and your new nephew. They went home a few moments ago."

"You got to babysit?"

"I babysat the other day. Today we talked about your father."

"Wish I'd been there."

For two months after Andrew died, Connor was unable to talk about his father. And to this day, he hides his grief behind a show of bravado. Hearing him say he wanted to talk about his father was a great relief. "You'll have lots of chance to talk about your dad at Christmas."

"Feel like taking a break from everything?"

Connor switched topics faster than he switched traffic lanes. "Are you making me an offer? It has to include Fergus, you realize that."

"Where we're going, your felonious feline can't come."

"Don't talk nasty about my cat. And where exactly are you thinking we might go? Why don't you come home instead?"

"Sorry to disappoint, but you need to get out of Dodge, and I have just the place."

Connor's computer business took him all over the world. "Don't keep me in suspense," I implored, so happy to be having this conversation with this crazy man who happened to be my son.

"How about flying off to Chile?"

"The Chile in South America?"

"One and the same."

That was the last place I expected him to say. Well, not the *very* last—Antarctica would win that designation. "When?"

"January. I need to fly down there for a couple of weeks, and it would give us a chance to live a little."

"You haven't forgotten I'm your mother, have you? I don't spend my evenings going to bars."

"You might enjoy a bar in Santiago. All those Latin men—you might get a whole new perspective on life."

I'm speechless at the notion of taking off to a country I've only ever read about.

"Still there?" Connor asked, a faint tinge of worry in his voice.

"Yeah, I'm here, and let me do an instant replay. You want me to go to South America with you in January. And you mentioned Latin men."

His deep, throaty chuckle reached out to me. "That about covers it. Once I've got my business done, we could play tourist while we're there—mountains, wineries, seashore, all sorts of wildlife. You'd have time to learn a little Spanish before we go."

I'd never just packed up and taken off in my entire life. *So why not now, with my son who'd traveled everywhere? I'd be perfectly safe.* "You're on. I'll have to get my passport renewed, and I suppose I'll need shots."

"Don't worry. We can work out the details later."

"Have son with big job, will travel, right?"

Connor's laughter warmed my soul. "That's the whole point of the trip to Chile. You and I *both* need to get a life."

"Oh, oh. Something happened in your love life?"

"What love life?"

"Okay, I'll read up on Chile. This could mean a whole new wardrobe," I said, making a mental note to go on the Internet and check the temperature of Chile in January.

"It could mean a whole new everything," Connor assured me.

"Love you," I murmured, my voice sounding thick in my ears.

"Love you, too," he said before he hung up.

Yes, my darling Connor embraced life with such enthusiasm. An enthusiasm that was sorely tested fifteen years ago.

I'll never forget the call we got that dark November evening when Connor was fifteen and hockey was his whole world. His injuries put an end to his dream of playing professional hockey. And that night at the hospital, for the first time in our marriage, I saw fear in my husband's eyes.

The struggle to remain calm and hopeful in the midst of the surgeon's dire prognosis of possible brain injury took every ounce of emotional strength we could muster.

I can still hear Andrew's words that night in the E.R. waiting room as we waited for the surgery on Connor's brain to undo the damage from hurtling headfirst into the boards. "We'll get Connor through this. We'll keep him safe and we *will* make him better. You'll see—he'll be fine. He's our son, and he will recover."

Sure enough he did—except for the limp and the need for a cane. And Connor being Connor, he never once complained.

CHAPTER SEVEN

THE NEXT MORNING I was up early and on the Internet, looking for information about Chile while I mentally went through my closets searching for clothes that would work for everything from the mountains to the beach.

I was surprised to discover that Chile is a huge country, with every type of climate imaginable. My next project was to borrow Spanish-language tapes from the library. But as much as I enjoyed researching Chile, I wanted to read Andrew's next letter. After saving several tourist sites as bookmarks, I shut down the computer.

Andrew had been very interested in Connor's computer business and what his work involved. If only Andrew had lived to retire, he would've been thrilled to take a business trip with his son.

Trying not to think about what might have been, I scooped Fergus into my arms and settled back in the chair behind Andrew's desk. At the sight of Andrew's familiar scrawl, loneliness rushed through me, making me squeeze Fergus tighter.

With a yowl of displeasure, my four-legged furball

leaped from my arms. I ignored his pleas to get back in my lap as I flattened the rumpled pages of the letter on his desk.

Dearest Emily,

It's early April and my treatments are over. I woke up feeling good this morning, so thankful for everything life has given me. I've been so lucky all these years!

From my office I can hear you in the kitchen getting breakfast ready. You stuck your head in here a few minutes ago to see what I felt like eating, and I was inordinately pleased to be able to tell you I wanted French toast and maple syrup. My mouth is watering just writing these words.

I remember all those Sunday mornings of French toast and coffee we shared while we read the newspapers, and the sheer delight of having Jonathan and the twins in the kitchen with us. So many memories... The awareness in your eyes when I kissed you before pouring a cup of coffee. The ease with which you made Sunday mornings a familiar event. But, most of all, how simply hugging you close could heat my blood.

And to think I let a stupid situation at work invade my life to the point where I questioned the value of those precious experiences.

I realize what I'm about to tell you is some-thing you'd rather forget, but I need to explain what was going on in my head during those hectic years when the law practice was booming, the kids were showing us how vulnerable we were to growing older, and I was doing my best to deny it all.

I was too busy to give the whole age thing much thought until my thirty-eighth birthday. I'd gone into work as usual and my secretary had a cake for me. The staff was pleasant in their teasing and congratulations, but when I looked around, there were only three of us who'd passed the thirty-five-year milestone. And I was one of them.

Suddenly, those long evenings at work seemed dull and pointless. And the newer lawyers coming into our growing firm were young, ambitious and determined to set the legal world on fire. I felt like an old uncle whom they tolerated, not the brilliant lawyer I believed I was.

Every night I worked late, there were half a dozen of the young associates there. One of these was Jennifer Sargent, a name you hate to see or hear, but please bear with me. Jennifer was determined to prove something to her father, the judge, and she sought my advice and help at every opportunity.

I was flattered. Not only was she attractive and pleasant to be with, she enjoyed my company. She wanted to be a good trial lawyer, and she was willing to work hard. A dedicated associate who was eager to learn was exactly what I needed in an associate.

It was all so innocent in the beginning, when our mutual love of the law provided us with hours of strategizing and planning for court appearances. It was exhilarating and I felt alive in a way I hadn't since I started in law.

Meanwhile, you were busy with hockey games, basketball, gymnastics and your volunteer work at the school, while I spent most of my time at the office. We talked so little, mostly about events going on around us rather than about us and how we felt. As my law practice became busier, I came to see myself as a lawyer first, a husband second.

It wasn't until Jennifer made a pass at me that I realized she wanted more than just an opportunity to prove herself. What we did next I had no business getting involved in, and what those months did to our marriage, Emily, was my fault and mine alone.

I regret what I did, and if I had to do it over again, it would never have happened. I would have been home with you and the children. I would have put you first no matter what. But now I will make it up to you as best I can by putting you and your feelings first through this scary time.

Love always,
Andrew

My hands shaking, I put the letter down. The memory of those days and nights when I was preoccupied by the fear that something was terribly wrong in my marriage flooded back.

Two nights in particular stood out, nights when I began to see how much our life together had changed… for the worse.

The ringing phone interrupts the bedtime story I'm reading to our rambunctious nine-year-old twins. "Daddy, Daddy," they scream in unison as they tumble off the bed and out of their bedroom.

"Wait a minute, you two," I call after them, despite the fact that I know how pointless it is. They've been restless this evening due to the longer spring days, and partly due to the sense of uneasiness we'd all been living with these past months.

Andrew hadn't been home one evening in four weeks—always an excuse, always a pressing court date. But he's promised to be here tonight in—I check my watch as I race for the phone—about twenty minutes.

I lift the phone from its cradle and before I can speak, I hear Andrew's voice. He's talking to someone, sounding annoyed and preoccupied. I immediately feel somehow responsible for his state of mind, mostly because Andrew has taken to re-minding me of what he calls the good old days, when we both had our separate careers. I assume he's missing the freedom of two salaries and no major financial commitments. But who knows?

"Emily, I'm still working on the Costain case for tomorrow, and I won't be done for at least another two hours."

I feel lonely and unappreciated, but because the twins are listening to every word I say to their father, I pull myself together. "We were going out for dinner this evening. I didn't take anything out of the freezer—"

"Don't worry about it. One of the associates is getting some takeout. I'll be home as soon as I can."

Disappointment follows its familiar path through my heart as I try to think of something upbeat to say.

"Are you there, Emily? The kids are all right, aren't they?"

He hasn't asked about me or how I'm feeling or what I'll have for dinner. "They're fine. We're *all* fine, thanks for asking," I snap.

"Emily, I'm sorry, please don't be angry. I'll be home in a couple of hours. Why don't you make yourself a drink and wait for me?"

Another night of waiting? Why is it always *me* who has to wait around for *him?* "Why should I? You'll be too tired and too uninterested in my life to stay awake longer than it takes to brush your teeth. Besides, I have no intention of becoming an alcoholic," I reply, feeling my chest tighten.

"Please don't do this," Andrew says barely above a whisper. I can hear the exhaustion in his voice, and it's an automatic reflex for me to make some soothing remark to help him get past these moments of unease between us.

But I realize I don't care anymore. I've spent far too many evenings alone as it is. Now I'm going to spend another. So I say nothing.

"Look, I have to be ready for tomorrow, I have no choice. There's no one else who can go to court with this. Emily, I need you to understand."

I'm already supposed to "understand" the new suits, the change in hairstyle, the early-morning running group—and now I'm to understand that he can't keep our date.

"What's to understand? You don't have time for me anymore," I answer, my mind screaming to say much more. But I'm afraid that if I bring up how I'm feeling or confront him about his indifference, he'll use his tact and charm to convince me that I'm overreacting.

"Emily, that's not fair. I don't have any other options. If only you knew how hard this is for me."

He hangs up before I can answer him with all the things I desperately need to say. Even though there's no point in arguing with a dead phone line, I ache to tell him what I think of him and his career. What I wouldn't give to have the courage to yell all the angry words I've been keeping inside me…

How long had this been going on? I can't re-member a specific day, only that our conversations have been ending the same way for far too long.

Andrew calls to tell me he'll be late yet again, I bury my disappointment beneath a question about when I can expect him home. I hang up the phone, put the kids to bed and eat alone. And tonight he's made another request for understanding softened, or so he hopes, by an apology. But all I'm left with is a deep-seated resentment of his career—and a growing dread that I have no real role in his life.

Despite the anger, I can't bring myself to say what really lies beneath everything that's been happening.

I'm afraid Andrew no longer loves me.

The next evening, I hire a babysitter and go downtown to Andrew's office, determined to persuade him to go to dinner with me so we can talk the way we used to.

I pull into the parking garage, and I'm about to get out of the car when I see Andrew coming from the elevator bank with one of his young associates: a beautiful blonde who's walking way too close to my husband. I watch in agony as he puts his arm around her shoulders, his lips brushing her forehead while his eyes sweep the parking garage before returning to meet her wide smile.

I lean back in my seat, whispering a silent prayer that he won't see me, that no one will witness my humiliation. When their laughter fades and is replaced by the sound of Andrew's Mercedes starting up, I close the car door and speed out of the garage.

Somehow I manage to drive back to the house,

park the car, pay the babysitter and make it upstairs to the bedroom I share with Andrew.

I wait, hiding beneath the covers, listening for the sound of Andrew's car. It's after three in the morning when he finally comes home. By then, I've made my decision.

Lost in my reverie, I didn't hear that someone was tapping on the window of Andrew's study. Remembering what Sam had said about the break-in, my heart jumped in my throat. Burglars don't knock, I chided myself as I scrambled out of the chair and crossed the room.

CHAPTER EIGHT

"JONATHAN, WHAT ARE YOU DOING out there?" I asked through the glass.

"Let me in and I'll tell you." He smiled, and it was as if Andrew was smiling at me.

"Have you forgotten where the door is?" I asked, giving him my raised-eyebrow routine.

"I tried the kitchen door, but it was latched and you didn't answer when I knocked. Your car's in the driveway." He shrugged and gave me a questioning glance.

This wasn't the time to tell Jonathan that since the break-in I'd become more security-conscious. I didn't want my son to have anything more to worry about. "I'll be right there." I met him at the kitchen door and hugged him tight. He hugged me back, his arms locked around me, his face buried in my neck, his arms almost rigid in their hold.

"What's wrong?" was on the tip of my tongue, but knowing my oldest son's pride, I didn't say the words. Jonathan would tell me when he was ready to talk. For now, he needed to hug me and that was more than okay.

"How was your flight? Did your meeting in Boston go okay?" I asked, wanting to eliminate the obvious concerns, but I could see by the way he held me that whatever the problem, he was afraid.

He gave me one last bone-crushing squeeze and let go. Without meeting my gaze, he dropped into a chair at the kitchen table. "The flight was great and my meeting went really well."

"I'm so glad." Still feeling the need to connect with him, I smoothed the shoulder of his jacket.

With a half smile, he said, "Mom, it's so good to be home. How're you doing?"

"Life's good. But Fergus is growing larger even as we speak. I may have to enroll him in Weight Watchers," I said, determined to keep it light, to play along until he told me what was worrying him.

"That cat won't be able to put one paw in front of the other if he keeps eating like this."

"I do what I can to hold the line on his food intake, but he outmaneuvers me by burning fewer calories."

"Face it, Mom. Your poor excuse for a cat is spoiled," Jonathan teased, his eyes regaining some of their usual sparkle.

"Jealous?"

"Absolutely." The beginnings of a grin moved slowly over his face.

"How about coffee?"

"Sure," Jonathan said, glancing around the kitchen.

"Before you ask, I haven't changed anything in the house. I can't decide what I want to do. But I've started going through your father's desk," I offered as I made the coffee.

"Need any help with Dad's office?"

I turned to look at my son, my heart swelling in my chest at the expression on his face—one I'd seen so many times when my firstborn believed he could make my life easier.

How often had he lifted huge bags of peat moss out of the back of the car when I was on some mad gardening scheme? How often had he brought things up from the basement for me?

I brought the tray of coffee to the table and sat down next to him. "I don't want you to do anything while you're here but enjoy yourself. You've done enough this week, and having you here is such a wonderful surprise. And then there's baby Andrew. Let's drop over there in a little while and see them."

"Did you tell Zara I was coming?" he asked.

I shook my head. "I wanted to. You don't know how close I came to saying something last night on the phone. Zara was chatting away about Andrew, how he was doing and how much she wished you and Connor could be here to see him."

"Yeah, secrets don't have much of a shelf life with you," he said, patting my hand.

"Would you like to call Linda before we go to Zara's?"

"No, I'll do it later. I need time… We both need time," he said halfheartedly, a sad expression on his face.

Jonathan rubbed his hands together slowly, deliberately, and I watched as I considered what he meant by that. My heart picked up speed the longer he sat there saying nothing.

"Jonathan, what's wrong?"

His jaw working as his eyes focused on some point over my shoulder, he took a deep breath and met my anxious gaze. "Linda and I aren't getting along."

"What do you mean?"

He looked at me, his eyes glistening. "My life is such a mess right now, and I don't know if I can fix it."

"How bad is it?" I felt as if some unseen force was squeezing the air from my lungs.

"We're talking about getting a divorce." He stared down at his hands.

In that moment, Jonathan looked so much like his father, and he was obviously in so much emotional pain. What should I say? How could I help him? I'd been through this. I knew what it took to survive.

"Are you seeing someone else?" Oh, no! Of course I'd have to say something stupid like that. I wanted to hit myself over the head. I didn't mean it for one minute. Jonathan would never… Yet I couldn't block the idea that Jonathan was his father's son. Did that extend to his personal behavior? Had the experience of losing his father changed how he saw his own life? He was clearly unhappy.

"Not me. Linda." He shrugged. "I can't be sure. She's been so distant these past few months, so angry and impatient all the time. We don't talk anymore and she says it's because I'm too preoccupied with my job. I want another baby, someone for Megan to share her childhood—like I had. Linda doesn't want more children."

"And what about you? How do you feel?"

"The firm's never been busier, and there's always a crisis to deal with. Linda doesn't seem to understand that I can't leave work on a whim." Jonathan looked me straight in the eye, and his pain was almost palpable. "I don't know what to do."

Of all the conversations in the world that I might've expected to have with my son, this wasn't it. Jonathan, the son who showed stability beyond his years, who stayed at his father's bedside every night for the last two weeks of his life, was facing something so painful, so soul destroying…and there was little or nothing I could do to ease his agony.

I wanted to hold him the way I used to when he was a kid and needed consoling. If only this could be fixed with a Band-Aid and a hug. But the man seated across from me—his facial expression tense and his eyes clouded with uncertainty—needed more than simple reassurance. He needed me to understand what he was going through.

Could I? Could I accept that a son of mine, especially *this* son, would consider a divorce when he was the child best able to remember what he lived through when his father and I separated? Or, like me, did he feel he had no choice but to separate?

A thousand questions flitted across my mind as I looked at him, questions about how their marriage had gotten to this point. How hard were he and Linda willing to work to salvage what they had? Had they gone for counseling? What did *he* want to do?

But whatever was going on between them was their problem to solve. "What about Megan?" I asked.

Tears swam in his eyes and he looked away. "I'll do everything I can to protect Megan. I love her so much."

I placed my hand over his. "I know you love Megan, and you'll take care of her. Whatever you need to do, I'm here for you. If you need to talk, I'm willing to listen."

He wrapped his hands around mine and I could feel them tremble. "Mom, the last few months have been hard, and so many times I've wished I could talk to Dad. I really miss him. I didn't want to burden you with my troubles," he said, misery in his voice.

"Please remember that you and Linda need to be honest with each other about how you feel. Spend time alone together and talk about what's bothering you. Don't let work pressures keep you from seeing what's important to your happiness. If you need me to keep Megan while you and Linda take a holiday, I'll do it."

"Thanks, Mom."

"And you could never be a burden to me. Besides, I'm a tough old bird." Well, not *old,* just a little worn around the edges. "Your dad and I managed to patch things up and go on with our lives. Maybe you and Linda will, too."

"We've tried counseling, but nothing seems to be working." His hands clung to mine.

Impulsively, I stood, grabbed my son and threw my arms around him, my tears dropping onto the top of his head. "I love you, and I wish I could fix this for you."

Jonathan hugged me back. "Like you did when I was a boy. Mom to the rescue. Half the kids in the neighborhood were afraid of you. Did you realize that?" he asked into my arm.

"No, I didn't, but they probably had reason," I said, stroking his head. "I had no use for kids who were rude."

"I can still see the look on Robin Sinclair's face the day you ordered him out of our tree house."

"He had it coming." I couldn't help smiling at the memory of Robin the Terrible, who thought nothing of cruising through my flower beds on his way to the backyard.

"Mom, are you sure you weren't a gladiator in another life?"

When I heard the teasing back in his voice, my arms shook with relief. "You're beginning to sound like those people with their reincarnation theories," I said, glad to see signs that his pain had eased. I let go of my son and slipped back into my chair.

"How about we head over to your sister's?"

Jonathan had his smile back. "Sounds great. I'll just put my bag upstairs."

He didn't have to ask where. I hadn't changed one

tiny thing in his room. I couldn't. Other people might say I was a possessive mother but I really didn't care. The house was mine, and there was no one else I was remotely interested in having in his room.

Jonathan did that long-legged skip of his as he came down the stairs, gave the newel post at the bottom of the steps a thump as he'd always done and strode along the hall into the kitchen.

"Are we ready to go?" he asked, grabbing the jacket he'd dropped on the chair earlier.

"Whenever you are—godfather."

WE ARRIVED AT ZARA'S house amid much hugging and laughter.

"I'm so glad to see you," Zara said, her arms around her brother, her cheek pressed to his. Knowing what might lie ahead for Jonathan, I memorized the smile of glee on his face as I watched him hug his sister.

These two had been close all their lives, and it made my breath catch to realize that so many years had passed and they hadn't lost that closeness, despite living so far from each other.

I knew with complete certainty that, thanks to Zara and her love and loyalty toward her brother, the distance would mean nothing if Jonathan needed her help and support through a divorce.

As we entered the living room, I saw a smile of welcome on Gregory's lips. "With Zara so busy with Andrew, I'm chief cook and bottle washer. And I'm beginning to like it. The clothes washer gave me a few problems, but I figured it out. I read the manual for the stove and cooked a chicken. It's nice to be able to help out, especially with Andrew. What can I get you?"

Would you believe it? My son-in-law doing kitchen duty? As long as I had known Gregory he'd seemed to spend all his time on his programming work, showing little interest in what went on around him. Obviously, all that had changed.

I pushed my surprise to the back of my mind and gave Gregory the once-over. He had dark circles under his eyes and kept glancing toward Zara with a look of pure wonderment on his face.

Gregory Cardwell taking charge. I liked it. "I'll have a cup of coffee if you have it."

"Coming right up."

I settled into the sofa, and as I sipped my coffee—very good coffee, by the way—I thought of the changes we'd gone through over the past few years. And despite everything, I felt great joy as I witnessed how happy Zara and Jonathan were to visit with each other.

A cry of distress from the baby monitor brought Gregory and Zara to their feet. "I'll go," Gregory said, heading for the stairs before Zara could respond.

When he came back down with Andrew cuddled against his shoulder, he gave a triumphant grin. "He was soaked. I had to change his diaper *and* his sleeper."

Zara winked at me as she motioned for her husband to pass the baby to Jonathan. A boulder-size lump closed my throat as my gaze held Zara's. Happiness was a living, breathing thing, an entity created by loving someone more than you love yourself.

The look in Zara's eyes told me just how much she loved her son, how completely love possessed her heart. In the exquisite moment of sharing a glance, we understood each other. We shared a common path in life, this child of mine and I.

After about an hour, Jonathan and Zara settled in for a long chat, while Gregory excused himself and went to his office in the basement. "Zara, would you drive Jonathan back when you're ready? I'm going home to get some rest."

"Mom, are you not sleeping well?" Zara asked, an anxious look back in her eyes.

"No, sweetie, I'm fine. Too much gardening the past few weeks, that's all." And Zara needed time with Jonathan.

I drove through the darkened streets, thankful that Jonathan was enjoying himself with his sister. He deserved every bit of happiness he could find.

The phone was ringing when I got in the door. I checked the number—Jonathan's in Bellingham. Afraid I might give some indication that Jonathan had confided in me, I made my tone purposefully upbeat. "Hi, Linda! How are you?"

"I'm okay."

"And Megan, is she there? I'd love to talk with her."

She didn't reply. "Is Jonathan around?" she asked instead. "I need to talk to him."

My daughter-in-law sounded as if she'd been crying. "Is anything wrong, honey?"

"I'm sorry to bother you, but I need to speak to Jonathan."

"Oh, Linda, he's not here. He's at Zara's."

"Will you get him to call me when he comes in?"

"Megan's all right, isn't she?"

"Oh, yes. I'm sorry. I didn't mean to worry you. Megan's fine. She and I were going to go to Seattle today, but there's been a change of plans."

Jonathan had said Linda was looking forward to visiting with her friend. What could have changed? "Why don't you call him at Zara's?"

"No, I don't want to interrupt his time with his godson. How is baby Andrew? I'm sorry I haven't had a chance to send a gift, but I will. I—"

I could hear Linda crying now. If only she was here with me. I could hold her, comfort her, make her feel less alone. Despite what was going on between them, she was my daughter-in-law and I loved her. "Linda, what's wrong? What can I do?"

"Nothing. I have to talk to Jonathan. But thanks anyway," she said, her voice shaking.

"Look, please call him. He won't mind, and neither will Zara. Please."

"I'll see."

Her call stayed in my mind long after she hung up.

An hour later, Jonathan came in the back door, whistling to himself. "Zara's so happy," Jonathan said, seeing me waiting in the kitchen.

I wanted to ask if he'd talked to Linda, but he deserved the chance to at least get in the door before I pressed him. "She and Gregory are both very happy and contented."

"Yeah, Gregory's so quiet most of the time, but he sure loves that baby."

Jonathan looked tired, which was hardly surprising given his busy week. I wondered if this was the time to mention Linda's call....

"Let's go to the living room," I said, wanting him to have a few minutes to relax.

"Okay."

Once we were sitting on the sofa, I looked at my son and my heart ached for him. How difficult it must have been to see his sister and brother-in-law so happy with a baby boy, when he wanted a son of his own. "How are you doing?"

"I'm okay. I was more worried about how you'd take my news."

Feeling bad that he was worried about me, I smiled to hide my sadness. "Did you make any plans with Zara?"

"Yeah. She wants me to spend the day with her tomorrow."

"That's wonderful."

Jonathan scrubbed his face with his hands, leaned back and stared at the ceiling. "Linda and I will work this out, one way or another."

"Of course you will. Just remember, if you need anything, I'm here."

I was about to ask if he'd heard from his wife when

he spoke again. "Thanks, Mom, but what I need right now is to hear how *you're* doing." Jonathan looked straight at me in his straightforward fashion, and I cringed. "Want to talk about the letters?" he asked.

"What about the letters?"

He touched my shoulder. "Mom, I'm so glad Dad left those letters for you—if you're all right with them."

"I am, truly. I've been reading one each day. I have to admit that early on, it was a little...disconcerting."

"And sad."

"Yes, that, too. But now it's easier, and I find your father's words reassuring. I'm sleeping better, too."

"That's good." Jonathan's expression said he wasn't reassured. "Zara's back on the subject of you buying a condo."

"She thinks I'm going a little strange living alone in this house."

"You're not, are you?" He peered at me with a macabre expression, making me laugh.

"No, silly. The only strange one in this house is Fergus."

"Promise?"

"Don't be smart," I kidded with him, still watching for any sign that he'd heard from Linda.

"I'm allowed. I'm the oldest. Speaking of that, I need to get some rest and so do you."

If, in fact, he'd had a disturbing call from his wife this evening, Jonathan seemed very calm. If he hadn't received one, she must plan to call here. My instinct told me that Linda was far too upset not to get in touch with her husband, regardless of what was going on in their relationship.

"I've got an idea. It's time to celebrate baby Andrew's arrival, just the two of us. Your father's Scotch collection is still in the liquor cabinet. Want one?"

"You're on."

I watched him move to the cabinet; the way he knelt down, turned the brass handle on the cabinet door and moved the bottles around while he made his choice was so like his father.

I couldn't tell him that. He'd be afraid I was about to launch into tearful memories, the way I had in the early months after Andrew's death, when I'd cling to Jonathan and tell him how much he reminded me of his father.

Jonathan returned with two crystal tumblers that Andrew kept with his Scotch whiskey collection. "Cragganmore, your favorite," he said, passing me a glass.

"To you and me, and to your father who kept only the best scotch in his cabinet."

"To us." Jonathan touched his glass to mine and sat down beside me.

A thumping noise erupted from behind the sofa. The window drapes swayed and Fergus appeared, his fur mussed and his eyes wide with indignation.

"Oh, yeah, I nearly forgot. To Fergus," I said, and we laughed in unison at my cat.

The ringing of the phone brought an abrupt end to our laughter.

"I'll get it," Jonathan said, jumping up and going to the kitchen.

I waited and waited and waited some more. I could tell that Jonathan's voice filled with disbelief, then what sounded like an attempt to be conciliatory, but I couldn't hear what he said. As much as I would've liked to know what was going on, I didn't go near the kitchen.

When he finally returned to the living room, his face was flushed, his eyes red rimmed.

I wanted to hug him, but I sensed this wasn't the time. "Was that Linda?"

He nodded, swallowing hard as he gulped the remainder of his Scotch.

"Jonathan, what happened?" I asked, seeing the look of sheer panic in his eyes.

"Mom, on top of everything else that's been going on with us the past few months, Linda hasn't been feeling well. She went to the doctor and he ran a bunch of tests." He turned to me. "We're expecting a baby next May."

I wanted to shout with joy at the prospect of another grandchild, but I could tell by his face that the news wasn't having the same effect on him—the person who should've been the most excited. "That's good news—isn't it?" I asked tentatively.

"Well, if we didn't already have marital problems, it might be." Jonathan rubbed his short-cropped hair, scowling anxiously. "But Linda doesn't want to be pregnant. She says our marriage isn't going to work out, and she's terrified of raising two children on her own." He took a deep breath

"After her dad left, her mom worked two jobs. Linda and Janice had to fend for themselves a lot. Linda has so many bad memories of those years, and she's terrified that she couldn't manage two children on her own."

"Surely she doesn't think she'd be a bad parent! She's well educated with a good income, and you'd be more than willing to share custody. You'd be there for her where the children are concerned, even if you weren't married. I mean, it'd be better if you could work out your problems, but if you can't, she'd be okay, wouldn't she?"

"Mom, a part of me is so excited, so thrilled about this. I want another child. But if a baby's only going to add to the list of problems we can't seem to solve, what am I going to do?"

I wasn't sure how to respond. This wasn't my life, my dreams for the future. "Jonathan, you have to have faith in your love for each other. You and Linda were deeply in love when you got married. It was obvious to everyone. Now you've hit a rough spot, and it'll take time and patience to see it through. But your love's worth it. Don't you believe that?"

"I want to believe it, but we're not even talking to each other anymore. I'm afraid she's going to insist… I feel as if I'm running out of options," he said, frustration showing in his voice.

"Would it do any good for you to go home tonight? If she sees you're willing to drop everything to be with her, maybe she'd be willing to talk this all out," I said, searching desperately for a solution that would get my son and daughter-in-law to come to their senses.

How could their marriage be over so easily? And with children involved, one of them unborn… Shivering, I took his hand in mine. "Jonathan, call her back and tell her you'll be there as soon as you can get a flight out."

His hand was limp. "I would, if she'd have me. But she's going to her sister's with Megan until Monday. She doesn't want to hear from me until she's had time to think over her 'options' as she calls them. I don't know what she means by that, but I have a pretty good idea."

"Then why did she call you if she didn't want you to come home? I don't get it."

"Neither do I. All I can say for sure is that I've got nothing to rush home for. She won't be there," he said, getting up and heading for his room.

CHAPTER NINE

JONATHAN WENT UPSTAIRS and I followed him, hoping to convince him to go home. He told me that being in an empty house would only make him feel worse than he did now.

This morning he came downstairs and announced that he was going over to Zara's. He didn't mention last night, and neither did I. Knowing Jonathan, he'd discuss all of this with Zara.

Feeling at loose ends, I took my cup of coffee and went into Andrew's office. Yesterday's letter had brought back a lot of memories of where our life had gone astray. Talking to Jonathan about his problems had made it even clearer—life could be so difficult if we lost sight of who we were and what made us truly happy.

With a feeling of trepidation, I settled into the chair, took out the next letter and began to read.

Dearest Emily,
It's a beautiful late April day, but I feel a terrible
need to revisit the months when we were separ-
ated. I can't seem to stop myself from worrying

that I may not get another chance to explain what was going on with me during those months.

I should've told you all this before, but I was afraid that if you were aware of the truth, of how stupid I'd been, you'd lose respect for me because I'd been so gullible.

The worst day of my life, ever, was the day I came home early to pick up my suitcase for a trip to Boston. You had your own suitcases, along with the children's toys and clothing, all lined up in the hall, and the car keys on the hall table. You told me you were leaving and taking the kids, that I could sell the house or do whatever I wanted with it.

I watched you leave with so much fear I could hardly breathe. There was nowhere to turn for advice, and Jennifer was making demands I couldn't meet. Refused to meet.

She wanted children, while I was losing mine. I brought the kids back here to visit each week, but it was so lonely without you. I can still see the haunted look in our children's eyes, a look I put there.

It was Sam who helped me see just how much of an idiot I'd been to let you leave. He showed me, too, how big a fool I'd been to even entertain the idea of having anyone else in my life. Some of those man-to-man talks we shared were pretty brutal, let me tell you. But I'll never forget how helpful he was to me when I needed advice on getting you back. What a true friend he was through those months…and now when I'm sick, he's been everything I could've asked for in a friend.

Emily, Sam Bannister cares about you, and he'll be there if you need him. He won't intrude on your life, but you can trust him.

Apart from your dad, I'd never had a friend like him. And I never will again.
Love always,
Andrew

Why was Andrew dwelling on those awful months? My mind circled the memories of the days and weeks after I'd decided to leave.

If it hadn't been for my Aunt Celia, I would never have survived. The day I landed on her doorstep, too overwrought and confused to make much sense, was so difficult.

She took the four of us in and provided a safe haven while I found a teaching job and attempted to create a normal life for the children.

All the while my life was falling apart. I was angry one minute, distraught the next, and in between I was fearful that what I was doing to my children would damage them forever.

Until the day Aunt Celia gave me her version of what she called "Marriage 101"…

The twins are in the den of Aunt Celia's sprawling bungalow doing their homework while

Jonathan is at basketball practice. Staying at Aunt Celia's meant the children didn't have to change schools—which is a relief—but I can't stay here much longer.

I need a place of my own, especially now that I have a teaching job—and a classroom full of fifth-grade children who keep me too busy to worry about what lies ahead.

Aunt Celia is the only one of my father's sisters who'd married, a marriage that ended when Uncle Herb died of pneumonia. She's been so helpful, reassuring me with soothing words.

Still, caring for three kids and their overwrought mother can't be easy for her.

"Emily, dear, this arrived in the mail for you today, from Pascal and Emmerson," my aunt says, coming into the kitchen, a look of apprehension on her face.

A law firm. My chest tightens as I take the envelope from her. I'm aware of the contents of the package; I hired the firm to act on my behalf. Seeing Andrew and Jennifer together that evening in the parking garage had confirmed my worst fear, and when I confronted Andrew about her the next night, he didn't deny anything.

"It's separation papers," I say quietly, not wanting the children to overhear my words or witness my sadness at seeing the official envelope.

"A separation agreement? What happened to Andrew's plea to see you, to talk about your situation?"

Aware that signing these papers would make our separation a legal reality, I fight back tears. "He wants to talk about getting back together, but I can't do it. *He's* the one who ruined our lives by having an affair, and now he wants me to believe him when he says he's sorry."

"You're hurt and I can understand that."

"He betrayed me with another woman! He didn't care how I felt, and I can't forgive him for doing what he did to me, to us."

"Dear Emily, have you thought this through?" my aunt asks, concern evident in her voice.

"It's all I ever think about, and I'm tired of it," I say defensively.

My aunt sighs. "Emily, sit down. We need to talk. Or at least I do."

I don't *want* to talk about it. Talk isn't the answer as far as I'm concerned, but Celia is all the family I have close by and I've come to rely on her support and advice. "I'm listening."

"For what it's worth, this is a mistake." She nods at the envelope. "In the past twenty years, I've had half a dozen friends go through a divorce, and all of them have ended up unhappier than they were in their marriages."

"But there's lots of reasons people aren't happy after a divorce," I say. "Maybe they weren't able to make it on their own, or maybe they got mixed up once again with the wrong kind of man."

"Or maybe they still loved their husbands and were too stubborn to admit it."

I don't need to hear this. Yes, I'm stubborn, but I'm not stupid. I pretend to study the diamond pattern of the tablecloth. "That's not how it is with Andrew and me. Andrew doesn't love me or he wouldn't have had an affair."

"Honey, this isn't about Andrew, it's about you and what you want in life."

Her words surprise me. This *is* about Andrew. Everything in my life has always been about Andrew.

Not anymore. "I want a divorce. Andrew gave me no choice."

"See, there you go, letting what Andrew did carry more weight than what *you* want—or need. You're a brilliant woman with a great future as a teacher. You love your life, your children, and I suspect you still love Andrew, despite the difficulties you've been through recently."

"This was Andrew's doing, not mine."

"Are you one hundred percent sure?"

I'm hurt by my aunt's words, and I fire back. "Andrew had the affair, not me! I was left to pick up the pieces on my own."

"Were you happy before you found out about the affair?"

I want to tell my aunt Celia what I'd told everyone else, about how my marriage would've been fine except for Jennifer. But this woman, who'd been with me through so many events in my life, deserves the truth. "I wasn't—but it was because I was alone all the time. We didn't talk very much. Andrew always had something going on."

"Why do you suppose that was?"

"Probably because we… I guess we didn't—"

"Did you hear the 'we' in what you said? You're including yourself in what happened."

"I didn't know what to do! And Andrew didn't try. A lot of people were aware of what was going on with Jennifer, and nobody bothered to tell me. It hurt to face friends, realizing that many of them had known about Andrew's affair long before I did." As I said these words, I was acutely aware of how much my pride had been hurt by his behavior.

"I understand," my aunt says softly.

"I wish all of this hadn't happened. But I can't change what's been done. How can I ever trust him again?"

"Marriage is about two people keeping the love between them alive. That means sacrifices on both sides. Yes, I can see how much he hurt you and how angry you are about it. But anger often hides fear, and you wouldn't be afraid or angry if *this* was what you wanted, if your life now was what you needed. If you ask me, you still love him, and you're afraid of what your life will be like without him. And if his conversations with me are any indication, he's desperately in love with you—and he's a man."

Surprised, I look at her. "What's that supposed to mean?"

"Men do the dumbest things when they're afraid of getting old. It makes them stupid where female flattery is concerned."

"Meaning?"

"Meaning, Andrew made a stupid mistake when he had that affair. A mistake that could cost him his home, his family but most importantly the woman he loves."

"He's the one who made the mistake, not me. And I'm not going to take responsibility for that."

"No, you didn't make that *particular* mistake. The mistake you're about to make is that you're going to let your pride get in the way of finding out if your marriage has a chance. Yes, what he did will take a lot of forgiveness on your part, and he'll have to work hard to earn your trust. But that's what marriage is all about, working to remain close and loving each other…despite the pain and hurt."

"So I'm supposed to forgive, forget and take him back?"

"All I'm asking is that you search your heart and be honest with yourself. Do you want a legal separation because you no longer love your husband and you plan to move on with your life? Or do you want it to prove that you can hurt him as much as he's hurt you? And be careful that in your need to hurt him, you don't hurt yourself more."

"So what are you suggesting I do?"

"If you want Andrew, fight for him. Don't walk away from your marriage and let the other woman be the last memory you have of your life together. And if you do decide to give him another chance, don't waste time looking back. Life's too short and too precious to let old hurts get in the way."

"What if you're wrong? What if we try again and a year from now I'm back here?"

"It could happen. No one can predict the future. But if I were you, I'd take a chance on him. It's worth the risk, if only to say goodbye to what the two of you had together."

Close to tears, I whisper, "Do you give this speech to all your friends and relatives?"

"No. I call this Marriage One-O-One, and it's for the people I love. I love you a great deal. You're the daughter I never had."

Aware from long experience that any show of affection will embarrass Aunt Celia, I squeeze her fingers. "I'll call Andrew, I promise."

And I did. A call that led to what we later dubbed the pimpmobile caper, which gave a whole new meaning to the word, surprise…

It's nearly seven in the evening, and my stomach feels like somebody's standing on it as I look out the window for Andrew's Mercedes. After Aunt Celia's talk, I called him. It had been such an awkward call, I nearly hung up. But finally we agreed to have coffee together.

I'd taken Aunt Celia's words to heart. Seeing the

stark vulnerability in Andrew's eyes as his fingers nervously rubbed the edge of his coffee cup convinced me to listen to what he had to say.

He wanted to take me out on a date. He said it was to make up for all the evenings I'd spent at home alone with the children. I said one date wouldn't even begin to make up for that, and he agreed. But he also said it's where we'd have to start.

So that's why I'm standing here staring out at the street. I agreed to go to dinner with him this evening. A trial run.

With my mind on meeting Andrew, I'm only half paying attention as I watch a white limousine ease to a stop at the curb.

The driver gets out, walks around the car and opens the door. Andrew appears from behind him and comes up the walk, a huge bouquet of yellow roses clutched in his hands.

Trying to understand why he arrived in a limo, I wait for the doorbell to ring. When I let him in I see the anxious look in Andrew's eyes and it makes me want to comfort him. But I'd been there, done that, and for what?

It's my turn to be comforted.

"Surely you don't expect me to go anywhere in that monstrosity, do you?" I ask.

"I'll explain everything later. These are for you," he says sheepishly.

"You never buy me roses."

Get 2 Books FREE!

Harlequin® Books,
publisher of women's fiction,
presents

HARLEQUIN®
Super Romance®

GET 2 BOOKS

We'd like to send you two *Harlequin® Superromance®* novels absolutely free. Accepting them puts you under no obligation to purchase any more books.

HOW TO GET YOUR
2 FREE BOOKS AND TWO FREE GIFTS

1. Return the reply card today, and we'll send you two *Harlequin Superromance* novels, absolutely free! We'll even pay the postage!

2. Accepting free books places you under no obligation to buy anything, ever. Whatever you decide, the free books and gifts are yours to keep, free!

3. We hope that after receiving your free books you'll want to remain a subscriber, but the choice is yours—to continue or cancel, any time at all!

EXTRA BONUS

You'll also get two free mystery gifts! (worth about $10)

FREE!

BUSINESS REPLY MAIL

FIRST-CLASS MAIL   PERMIT NO. 717   BUFFALO, NY

POSTAGE WILL BE PAID BY ADDRESSEE

Harlequin Reader Service

PO BOX 1867

BUFFALO NY 14240-9952

NO POSTAGE
NECESSARY
IF MAILED
IN THE
UNITED STATES

"It's the new me."

He shifts from one foot to the other, and I want to put him out of his misery, but why should I? Sure, I'm being difficult, but I figure I'm entitled.

And that vehicle at the curb… "You'd better come in before one of the neighbors starts a rumor about my aunt winning the lottery."

He follows me into the living room, and I take the flowers and find a vase for them. When I return, he's studying the limousine.

"So that's part of the new you, as well?" I ask, nodding toward the vehicle hogging the narrow street.

He turns to me, a determined set to his jaw. "Yes, it is. I want us to put the past months behind us and have a night of fun. I've been working like a dog, living in that ark of a house by myself and missing my family so badly I can't sleep. But most of all I've been missing you."

His words slam into my heart, words I'd lost hope of ever hearing. But missing me is not enough. Who wouldn't miss a wife who looked after everything from dental appointments to getting the car serviced to balancing the checkbook? "It's too bad you didn't show a little more appreciation for what we had when we still had it."

"You'll never know how much I regret having anything to do with Jennifer," he says, his eyes holding mine with a longing that makes me want to run into his arms.

Too soon, way too soon. "So you want to go out on the town tonight?" I ask, moving out of his reach. I don't trust myself any more than I trust him—but for entirely different reasons.

He extends his hand. "I want to have dinner with you and then go dancing."

"You *are* desperate," I say before I can stop myself.

He laughs. "Definitely desperate. And you probably think I've lost it completely with the limousine, right?"

His laughter brings me back to the good times when we'd share a bottle of cheap red wine and watch some sitcom on TV. "Yes, I do think you're crazy, but I'm here and you're here, so what's next?"

"A client of mine owns the thing, and you and I deserve to live a little. Have you ever gone anywhere in a limousine? I haven't."

He has a point, and if we don't get that vehicle out of the neighborhood soon, my aunt will be the subject of gossip for weeks. "Okay, let's go."

He helps me on with my coat, and his hands brush my shoulders. Too afraid I'll do something foolish—like wrap my arms around his neck—I fiddle with my evening bag.

The driver holds the car door open and we slide into the backseat. Miles of gray-blue leather, soft lights and music greet us.

"So what do you think?" Andrew asks.

"I think I'll reserve my opinion for once," I say,

rubbing the leather. "Isn't there supposed to be a liquor cabinet? That's what they show on TV."

Andrew and I are peering around the interior when a voice comes out of the wall. "Where to, sir?"

Andrew looks at me. "I have a reservation at Sartres, but it's your choice."

I'm tempted to agree…to see and be seen with my husband at the best restaurant in Portland, but this is *my* night. "What if I said I want to go to Boston for the night?"

"Done."

"You're kidding, of course."

"Boston it is," he says to the driver, and we glide away from the curb.

"Wait. I didn't realize you were serious, but if I can go anywhere…let's drive to Old Orchard Beach. It's only a few miles from here."

He hits a button and tells the driver while I look around in awe at the opulent interior. "What's in here?" I ask, opening the door to a fridge—finding champagne and strawberries.

My husband, a romantic? "This is too much."

Andrew pulls out a bottle of very expensive-looking champagne and takes two flutes off the polished wooden shelves beside the fridge. The cork pops, flies to the ceiling and falls to the floor.

Champagne, a limo and the music of Tommy Dorsey. I have to hand it to Andrew, he's doing it up right, I muse as I sip my champagne. Oh, and does it ever taste good! I take a bigger sip. Another glass of this and I'll be asleep or silly.

My glance shifts to Andrew and he's looking at me with the oddest expression on his face. "Are you okay?" I ask.

"I haven't been this okay for months."

I don't know how to respond to this, and I usually manage to put my foot in it when I'm nervous, so I busy myself by discovering all the gadgets lining the inside of the limo.

I spot a pop-out area on the console between the seats and press the button. A panel slides away, displaying condoms in every color of the rainbow. Unable to resist, I pick up a couple of the fluorescent ones.

"What have we here?" I ask, caught between surprise and curiosity. Andrew has never worn a condom in his life, at least not in his life with me.

"What the hell—" He stares at the condoms and back at me.

"What exactly does your client use this vehicle for?"

"He has a fleet of airport limousines. This is one of them."

"You're sure?" I ask, pulling open the drawers that line the area on the other side of the fridge. "What's this?" I pull out a bunch of glossy magazines with big-breasted women adorning the covers. "Your new taste in reading?" I ask, beginning to enjoy myself.

Andrew looks like he's been hit by a brick. "Emily,

I had nothing to do with this." He grabs the magazines from my hands and tucks them out of sight.

The genuine embarrassment on his face makes me want to hug him. But I don't. Not a good idea. "I know you didn't. And I have seen those magazines before, you know. I've got a teenage boy in the house and I'm not a complete prude."

He sighs and studies his hands. "But you finding stuff like that was hardly how I envisioned our evening."

He's trying to make things right, and I'm being flippant. I watch the bubbles gather on the inside of my glass, and suddenly what I want is a chance to really talk. "Ask him to pull over."

Andrew looks at me for a moment and then does what I ask.

"I'm aware that you planned a special night for us, and it is. But is all this for me, or has your new life lost its charm?"

I hear his sudden intake of breath as he shifts uncomfortably in the seat. "Emily, I want you back home with me. I love you. I can't make my life work without you. If I could take back what I've done, I would in a heartbeat. I can't. So I'm asking for a second chance."

I close my eyes and listen to his words, and all I can think of is how much I miss having him near me, having his full attention like this. "And what happens the next time you meet someone you're attracted to?"

"There won't be a next time. I promise you." He reaches for my hand, and I let him touch me.

How I want to believe him, to feel loved and cared for the way I once did.

What do I feel at the moment? Anxious. Lonely. Afraid a reconciliation might fail. Then I see my life stretching ahead of me, a life without Andrew. A life where the children continue to ask for their father the way they have every day since we separated.

They miss him. Zara cries herself to sleep while Connor insists on sleeping with me. Jonathan is having trouble at school. I look at this man who's been my life for so long, and I realize how strong my feelings for him are. I am deeply hurt by what he did, but I still love him. "What are we going to do? How do we get back what we lost? I can't forget what you did to me, to our children. I don't know how to trust you again."

Andrew brings my hand to his chest. "Emily, I'll do everything I can to convince you that I'm sincere when I say I love you and want you back. But if this doesn't work for you, I'm willing to do whatever I can to make you happy without me."

This man I've spent so much of my life with is completely sincere. I see it in his eyes. "How do we find out if this is going to work?"

"Come home with me. Tonight." He pulls me to him, his lips searching for mine, his body curving toward me in that old familiar way.

I want him to hold me and say that everything

will be fine. I want him to make love to me, right here and now. I put my arms around his neck. He kisses me and I kiss him back.

His groan of pleasure fills me with longing. I curl into his body, seeking his warmth and reveling in his scent. He lifts me up, his body sliding under mine as he presses me against him. His hands move urgently down my back.

"Andrew." His name comes out as a groan.

His hands are urgent, his fingers electric, and a sense of wonderment claims me. After all this time and everything that's happened, we still want each other.

Andrew slips his finger under my silk top, unhooks my bra.

I want to sink into his warmth, enjoy the excitement of his touch, his body pressed to mine. It's been so long…

But the sound of an engine and the scrape of boots on gravel make me open my eyes.

Lights flash. Doors slam. The door behind Andrew opens and we nearly land on the ground. "What the devil?" Andrew mutters.

I clutch his shirt, my heart pounding at the sight of a police car and a patrolman scowling down at us.

"Out of the car," he orders, flicking his flashlight over us.

Andrew groans, but this time it's not in the throes of passion. "Sit up, honey." He eases me off him and I begin to giggle nervously. Someone caught us making out like a pair of teenagers.

My giggling stops when I see the stern expression on the officer's face. I scramble to straighten my clothing when my fingers catch on part of my free-floating bra, loose somewhere behind my top.

I'm too shocked to say anything as we climb out of the car. I can imagine what my aunt will say if this makes it into the papers.

We stand like two condemned prisoners, leaning against the side of the limousine. I squint in the glare of the flashlight, looking for the handiest cover, only to discover a second police car parked by the side of the road.

"You're under arrest," the officer says as the driver is ordered out of the car.

"Arrest? What's the charge?" Andrew asks with indignation in his voice, all of which is wasted on the officer.

"Prostitution."

As I sat staring at Andrew's letter, I smiled at the memory. We were saved a trip to the precinct when one of the officers in the other vehicle recognized Andrew from court. I shuddered at what might have happened had there been any newspaper people around to report that a prominent lawyer and his estranged wife had been picked up on prostitution charges.

The owner of the limo had apparently rented the car we were in to a regular client of his. It had been under surveillance for several weeks, and it was our bad luck that we were in the wrong limo at the wrong time.

Andrew's client fell all over himself to make up for the mistake. And a week later Andrew and I had a beautiful trip to Old Orchard Beach and a long weekend in Boston, compliments of the owner.

I won't say that our weekend away was the turning point, but our shared laughter over the incident went some distance to heal the rift between us. And neither of us ever looked at a limo on the street again without chuckling.

We mended our relationship. It wasn't perfect, but possibly better in some ways than before Jennifer Sargent entered our lives.

In the years after our limo adventure, we were much more open with each other, less likely to let something go if it bothered us. It meant we argued more, but that helped us stay connected.

And now, realizing that Jonathan might be headed for divorce, I was overcome with foreboding. If Andrew were here to talk to Jonathan, to give him advice and a male point of view, things would be better.

Jonathan needed his father more than ever now, but Andrew was gone and there was nothing any of us could do to change that.

Least of all me.

CHAPTER TEN

LATER THAT MORNING AS I sat in the gazebo, I decided I needed a distraction from my worries and the memories I'd revisited in the past couple of days.

I was going to the kitchen for a cola when I spotted Sam on his hands and knees, digging around the roses draped over his bamboo trellis.

Remembering what Andrew had said about Sam made me think about the possibilities. Could *Sam* help Jonathan? He'd spent hours listening to Andrew pour out his marital problems. Sam had obviously given Andrew good advice. Did I dare approach him for advice, too? Perhaps he could tell me how to offer support to Jonathan. I couldn't ask him to talk to Jonathan, they weren't close enough for that. But I had to do something, if only to ease my own mind.

Before I could come up with a dozen reasons why I shouldn't, I crossed the lawn.

Now that I was standing in front of him, I felt silly. I'd never come into his yard like this before, although once in a while I had to chase his poodle to the hedge.

Sam sat back on his haunches and stared up at me. "I saw your car leave quite a while ago with Jonathan at the wheel. I take it he's off to visit his sister," he said, his face mostly hidden by a huge straw sun hat, which was coming apart.

Sam had to be the only person on earth who wore such an absurd hat, I mused as I knelt down next to him. "Yes." I smiled. "Zara's so proud of Andrew and so happy. What a wonderful time in her life."

"It is, and everything to look forward to. Now, what about you? How are you feeling?"

Did I dare confide in him about Jonathan? As I looked into Sam's eyes, I reminded myself that Andrew had suggested I could approach this man— my longtime neighbor and one of his closest friends— for help. But did I have any business meddling in my son's life? Not likely. Looking for a way out of this quandary, I kept my response light. "Oh, I'm feeling pretty good. Most of the time."

"Just not today, right?" Under the wide brim of his hat his perceptive eyes held such kindness and caring it pushed the air from my lungs.

Andrew's letter and Jonathan's personal problems hung around me like a dark cloak as I met Sam's gaze. The soft breeze stirred the rose-scented air as I struggled with an urgent need to confide in the man my husband had trusted all those years. "How could you tell?"

"You're easy to read," Sam said as his hand covered mine. I felt the leathery warmth of his skin, the way his body leaned toward mine.

"Yeah, I'm worried about Jonathan," I said frankly.

"He and Linda are having problems, and Jonathan needs his father's advice."

"And you're feeling helpless."

Tears stung my eyes. I glanced away, studying the trellis as I fought to hold my feelings in check. Unable to answer without crying, I simply nodded.

"I'm a pretty good listener, if you'd care to talk," he said as his arm settled on my shoulders. "And I'm always available," he offered, his face near mine.

Unable to resist his warmth and the scent of earth and sun that clung to his skin, I moved closer. He slid his arms around me, shielding me from all my worries, and for a few welcome moments I didn't feel so alone.

And oh, how wonderful it felt to have a man's arms around me, to feel his breath on my cheek. I'd missed this feeling of protection, of caring…the silent communication that had been such an important part of my life.

I noticed the dappled light of the garden, the muted hum of a bee, as he held me.

I wanted to bury my face in his chest and stay there. I wanted to forget all my worry over Jonathan, my longing for Andrew. I wanted…what did I want?

A car horn broke the spell.

"Mrs. Arnold's waving at us," Sam said, pulling away.

"The same Mrs. Arnold who reported a couple of kids for necking in the park," I muttered, feeling as if I'd been caught in bed, rather than in the garden, with Sam.

Silly!

Yet the stiff set of Sam's shoulders, told me he felt it, too. Standing up, he held out his hand.

"Have you heard back about the fence estimates?" I asked, ducking my head to hide my embarrassment, while I surreptitiously glanced down the street. Molly Arnold was nowhere in sight.

Sam cleared his throat nervously as he picked up his trowel. "I got estimates from four different companies. In my opinion, our best bet is a black steel fence. There are several designs and different weights of steel. Want to see the brochure?"

He looked at me with such attentiveness I felt connected to him again. "No, I'm willing to go with whatever you decide," I said, fighting an awkwardness I hadn't experienced before.

"You're sure?"

"I trust you to pick what we need, and besides, it was your idea. I don't know anything about fences and I don't want to learn. Just tell me what my share of the cost is."

"I'll do that. But I can't imagine you not wanting to learn something. Aren't you the one who taught Andrew all about transplanting shrubs?"

"Yeah, but he asked for it by hanging around me when I was gardening."

"That wasn't his version of things. According to him, your gardening was a pleasant distraction from all his work concerns." Sam fidgeted with his trowel. "I'm sorry, I didn't mean to remind you—"

"It's all right."

His face brightened. "So we can make our plans?"

"Our plans?"

"The dance class. Are you still up for it?"

I saw the smile in his eyes, the way he looked at me. The beginnings of a blush started up my neck. This was about more than comfort and advice… "Are you sure you want to take dance lessons with me? You're not just being kind because you feel sorry for me?"

"Not a chance," he said with a grin. "Kind doesn't cut it when my whole reputation as a Don Juan is at stake."

I grinned back.

"Is that a yes?"

I had to hand it to him; although he seemed awkward and disheveled, he understood how to close a deal. But did I mind? Not really. If my new life was going to begin with flying off to Santiago, Chile, for heaven's sake, why shouldn't I take up ballroom dancing? "Yes. It's a yes."

He dropped his trowel and grabbed my hand. "This calls for a celebration. Come on around to the patio and have a glass of my homemade wine."

I was inordinately pleased by the feeling of my hand in his. "Isn't it a little early for alcohol?"

"Is the sun over the yardarm?" Sam glanced at his watch and squinted up at the sky.

"It's only eleven-thirty."

"Close enough," he said, leading me to the back of his house. Sam's poodle, Bouncer, barked at us from the living room window. "Your dog needs to speak with you." I kidded to cover my nervousness.

"He'll be fine. I walked him earlier, and he's had his lunch. It's time for his afternoon nap."

I suspected that Sam cared as much for Bouncer as I did for Fergus. I'd seen him out many mornings walking his dog when Andrew left for work.

Sam's garden at the rear of the house glowed with huge red, green and blue pots brimming over with plants of all colors and shapes, set off by beautiful copper irises standing tall at the back of each container, the sun glinting off their hammered surfaces. Happy-faced sweet peas sprawled over the wall next to the patio doors.

"Have a seat and I'll be right back."

Before I could get comfortably settled in the wicker chair he'd returned with fluted, long-stemmed glasses edged with gold and filled with a pale, pink liquid.

"This is a sparkling wine kit I decided to try. It's wonderful on warm days like this. Taste it." He passed me a glass before he disappeared into the kitchen again. He came out with a tray of cheese and crackers.

"Lunch?" I asked.

"By all means," he replied, stretching his long frame over the chair next to mine.

We sat in comfortable silence while we sipped the wine. I don't know what I'd expected, but certainly not the bubbly tartness as the wine tingled its way down my throat. Feeling pleasantly warmed by the wine and the sun, I leaned back and stared up into the canopy created by the tall oak trees along the far edge of his patio.

"Ah, this is the life, isn't it?" Sam asked.

"There's something so peaceful about being out here under the sun, drinking wine. I haven't felt this good in…a long time."

"I'm pleased to hear you say that."

I heard a funny catch in his voice and looked at him. "Are you fishing for a compliment?"

His gaze met mine. "A compliment wouldn't go astray."

My heart bumped my rib cage. "Okay…you're the best gardener on Postmaster Lane."

I watched him as he tipped his hat back from his face and held his glass up to the light. "Thank you. I make great wine, as well."

He glanced over the rim of his glass at me, searching my face. An unfamiliar sense of excitement had me tightening my grip on the wineglass.

What are you doing? You're too old to be carrying on like this!

"Let's eat, I'm starving," I said, shifting my attention to the rim of my glass and keeping it there.

"What about the wine?" he asked, moving the plate of crackers and cheese closer to my side of the table.

"Your wine is wonderful. Truly wonderful."

"Thank you. This is my lucky day. I get to drink wine with a beautiful woman while I enjoy her compliments."

"You're smooth, I'll give you that," I said, feeling the buzz of the wine and a reckless need to flirt—with Sam of all people.

"Well, now that I have you where I want you…"

I nearly jumped out of my chair.

"Sorry, I was only teasing, but this time I need *your* advice."

"I'm not available for advice-giving today. Try tomorrow." I was about to launch into the cost of my advice and a lot of other silliness when it dawned on me. For the first time since Andrew died, I was teasing a man and enjoying it. He smiled at my remarks but I could see that he'd grown serious.

"I do actually need your advice," he said. "Robert's coming over this evening, and I want to talk about Phillip. I don't know how to approach my son. Robert doesn't believe there's a problem with Phillip. My son was slow to read and still reads very little. He thinks I'm overreacting, and trying to prove that he's not responding to Phillip's needs." He turned the wineglass gently in his hands. "Maybe he's right. When Robert was in school, he always tuned me out when I talked about his poor grades, and now I'm afraid he'll tune me out again. Only this time an innocent little boy will lose out."

My eyes met Sam's and the uncertainty in his gaze created a bond between us. Emily Martin, widow, mother, grandmother, teacher, volunteer and so-so bridge player was genuinely needed here.

I placed my wineglass on the table. "You know what I'd do if I were you?" I asked.

"Tell me. I need all the advice you can offer."

"I'd encourage Robert to find someone to help Phillip

with his reading. Someone who has the time to spend with him, encouraging him to overcome his problem. You could start now and continue until he's assessed for any underlying issue that might be affecting his ability to read."

"Are you volunteering?"

Was I? Zara had suggested that I should. If I did, I'd be around Sam a lot more often, and I wasn't quite ready for that—at least not yet. "I'm not sure, but I'll help you get his assessment organized in the meantime."

"You know what, Emily? You don't give yourself near enough credit."

I glanced at him, at the man who a few weeks ago was way down on my list of the people I wanted to spend time with. "What do you mean?"

"I mean you're a very smart woman, and Andrew was a very lucky man. In fact, he told me so on a number of occasions."

His words flustered me, but the sincerity in his eyes made me feel valued…special. I could really get to like this man, and if we *were* going to be spending more hours in each other's company, that wasn't a bad idea. I thought of the impending dance lesson.

LATER, AS I WALKED BACK across the yard toward my own house, I recalled the lunch we'd shared, the delicious gazpacho soup he'd served. I smiled at the way we'd laughed at the same silly jokes, gossiped about the neighborhood, but most of all, how nice it felt to be appreciated.

CHAPTER ELEVEN

BACK IN THE HOUSE, I was struck with the need to read
another of Andrew's letters. Was it because of my en-
counter with Sam? Was I feeling guilty? Right now, it
didn't matter. All that mattered was my urgent need to
connect with my husband.

I reached the office and settled into the chair.

Dearest Emily,

*I'm sitting here staring at the bouquet of May
flowers you picked along the edge of the ravine
the other day.*

*I know you've probably heard enough about
how sorry I am for the affair. But I need to tell
you something. That night in the limo—the way
we stood together while the police questioned us
was the final turning point for me. No matter
what situation I had to face, I'd rather have you
beside me than anyone else in the world.*

*Jennifer Sargent meant nothing to me and
never had. My insecurities were the reason for
that relationship, and you faced the conse-
quences of my actions without flinching.*

I was completely panicked by the idea that if you'd refused to see me that night, or had found someone else, my life would never be the same.

I decided as we stood by the limousine that if we had a second chance, you'd never again have to worry about anything that was within my power to influence. Your life with me would always be one of love and security. I would be there for you.

When we first got back together, I realized you were waiting for me to tell you what I've just written, but I couldn't bring myself to say the words.

I let pride stand in the way.

Without your courage, your willingness to try again, I don't know what would have happened. I want you to understand that I regret my stupidity, and never more than in the last few months.

Thanks, my love.

And now I need to get back to the veranda to work on the crossword puzzle in today's paper. I don't feel like doing much these days. I see in your eyes and the way you give me small chores like shelling peas for dinner, that you're trying to keep me from feeling useless.

I can no longer deny that my body is growing weaker, and the bouts of nausea have become more frequent. I can imagine your words when you read this, how you'll be upset that I didn't tell you more about what I was feeling.

But I promised myself that I'd protect you and

give you the best I had to offer while I could.
There's nothing I can do to stop the inevitable,
but I will do what I can to ease your worry.

Emily, I want you to remember how much I
have always needed you in my life, how loving
you has made me complete.
Love always,
Andrew

Driven by emotions I couldn't control, I reread the letter. His need to protect me after we got back together became so much a part of our relationship, from the way he took over around the house, arranging appointments to have repairs done, to the way he looked after all our financial matters and paying the bills.

He took me on a date every weekend, often simple trips like going to the zoo or for a long walk in the woods, dates that were the best of our time together as a couple.

Feeling the need for air and space away from my memories, I went out the back door and into the light of late afternoon.

Relief whistled through me at the sight of Sam in his yard, digging up the hedge in preparation for the new fence. Without a sideways glance, I charged across the lawn. "Oh, I'm so glad you're out here," I said.

He stopped shoveling, his eyes searching my face. "Emily, what is it?"

"I'm not sure anymore. I mean, I've been reading letters Andrew wrote me before he died."

He sighed, and a slow, sad smile crept over his face. "You're finally able to read his letters."

"I just found them in his desk drawer. Did you know about them?"

"I knew Andrew was writing you letters, but I had no idea where he left them."

"Why did he tell you?" I asked.

Sam looked away. "Probably because we were close friends, and had been for years. And in those last months, Andrew carried so much guilt about having an affair that he wanted to leave you something that was yours alone."

"Did he tell you what was in the letters?"

"No, of course not."

"Why didn't he tell me?" I demanded, feeling left out and ignored. "If only he'd been willing to say these things to me, if only he hadn't left those feelings for a letter…"

"Look, this isn't an easy topic for either of us, but you have to understand something. When Andrew got involved with Jennifer Sargent, it had nothing to do with you."

"It had everything to do with me, and with our children," I said angrily. I instantly regretted blurting out those words because for the first time since I'd known Sam, what he thought of me mattered.

"I meant it had nothing to do with how good a wife and mother you were. None of it reflected badly on you, only on him. You were the love of his life."

Sam's voice was gentle as he edged closer.

I stepped back. "Go on."

"I doubt Andrew ever talked much about how lonely he was over there without you." Sam nodded in the direction of my house. "He would've given up everything he had to get you back. As I listened to him talk, I realized that a love like the one you and Andrew shared was a precious gift. And no one had the right to get in the way of such love," he whispered, his hand touching my shoulder.

The heat of his body surrounded me. The smell of cedar and his sweat drew me to him. "I need to tell you something," he said, his lips just inches from mine.

Was he going to kiss me?

"What?" I asked in a breathy tone I didn't recognize.

"I've envied Andrew and his second chance at love…with someone like you," he said, a look of naked vulnerability in his eyes.

His words hung suspended between us. Could I let myself believe what he'd said? Could I trust him? "You're not saying that because you feel sorry for me, are you?" It sounded absurd to my anxious ears, but Sam's response had had that effect on me.

"I definitely do not feel sorry for you," he said, sliding his arms around me. Holding me close, he kissed me, a kiss that was tentative at first. Surprise and pleasure raced through me as I pressed my lips to his, opening my mouth in answer to the urgency of his kiss, the feel of his hands moving down my body.

The world slipped sideways. Physical need swept through me as Sam held me in his arms.

A car door slammed. The sound of feet smacking the pavement was followed by Zara's voice, emanating shock and disbelief. "Mom, what are you *doing?*"

We jumped apart, our joint embarrassment leaving us momentarily speechless. Sam looked down into my eyes, his voice tender. "Your mother and I were sharing a quiet moment together."

"I can see that," Zara grumbled.

"You don't believe your mother's entitled to moments like this one?" Sam asked, a smile crinkling the corners of his deeply blue eyes.

I didn't have to look to know that both Zara and Jonathan were staring at me. And I had to admit that, after the past few months, seeing me kissing a neighbor—*this* neighbor—would come as a shock. It was a bigger shock to me…but okay.

"I'll see you later," I said to Sam before heading across the grass to where Zara and Jonathan were standing shoulder to shoulder.

Feeling a little awkward, but not enough to regret kissing Sam, I went to the back door. "You decided to leave the baby home with his dad, did you?" I said, hoping to change the subject.

They followed me into the kitchen, where Jonathan angled his arms out of his jacket, a sheepish look on his face, and Zara plunked her purse on the table.

"Jonathan's going to drive me back in a little while. I can't stay long, but we wanted to talk to you, Mom." Her glance moved past me to her brother. "And even more so after what we just witnessed."

"How so?" I asked, still feeling Sam's kiss on my lips.

They slid into chairs across from each other, which guaranteed that I'd be sitting between them at the end of the table. Neither said a word, but I knew from the way Jonathan shuffled his feet under the table that he was ill at ease.

"Would either of you like some juice? Coffee?"

"Orange juice," Jonathan said, turning from me to Zara.

"I'll have a glass of water," Zara said, getting up and going to the sink.

I tried to make eye contact with Jonathan, but he wouldn't look at me. "So, let's hear it," I said, bringing him his juice. Suddenly I wanted to get the inevitable questions about my relationship with Sam out of the way.

"Mom, what were you doing kissing Sam Bannister of all people? He was Dad's friend, not yours. You don't even like him."

"This has nothing to do with your father. Sam and I are friends who enjoy each other's company."

"It looked like more than that to us," Zara said, her eyes swerving to Jonathan. "Is this what happens when you live alone?" Zara asked.

"I've lived alone for over a year, and I've kissed Sam Bannister once," I said, feeling the need to defend myself to my children. But I was pretty certain the two of them had something else on their minds. With Zara back in her chair and sipping on her water, I decided to come straight to the point. "But that's not why you came. You want to discuss how I should get on with my life."

Zara clasped her hands together. "It's true we've been discussing your situation." She exchanged glances with Jonathan. "We agree that you should sell this house."

"You *what?*" I choked. I was prepared to be told to "get a life" as they called it, but not this.

Jonathan and Zara watched me anxiously. "Mom, this is too much house for you to look after. Do you realize how many chores there are to be done around here? You can't possibly do all this on your own," Zara said, her accusing tone taking me by surprise.

"I don't see why not. Your father left me a list of who to call, and what to do," I said indignantly, yet inside I was writhing against the hard weight of insecurity in my stomach. After our separation, Andrew had taken over most of the responsibility and planning required to maintain the house until he was too ill to do it. While he was sick, I managed as best I could with Andrew's advice and input. But now I no longer felt capable because there was no one to help me, no one to talk to about the house. I couldn't impose on Sam. It wasn't right. He wasn't responsible for me. Yet living alone was so difficult…so lonely.

"Zara's got a point, Mom. This is too much house for you."

"I can't leave home…your home."

"But you're alone, and if anything should happen…"

And that break-in last week, practically in your back-yard. What if the burglars break in here next? Mom, I don't mean to upset you, but you have to face reality. The neighborhood's changing," she said.

"We're just concerned for you, Mom," Jonathan offered, his voice low, conciliatory.

Zara placed her hand firmly on mine. "I've been on the Internet checking on condos. I've got the names of a couple of Realtors we can talk to about listing the house."

"I've told you before, Zara. You don't have to worry about me. I'm fine. I love this house, and I won't listen to any more talk about leaving it," I said stubbornly. But I had a right to be stubborn. I would prove them both wrong.

Zara's cheeks flared pink. "You're not being fair. The three of us worry—"

"Zara, I'm fine. In fact, I'm going to Chile with Connor in January."

"Going to Chile? Mom! Do you have any idea how long a flight that is?"

"So it's a long flight. I'll have Connor with me. What's the big deal?"

"The big deal is that Connor isn't here when things go wrong. Connor just swings through, full of fun and without a care in the world. When he's gone and you're feeling lonely and missing Dad—" Her voice shook as tears pooled in her eyes.

Jonathan reached across the table and folded Zara's hands into his. "It's okay, Zara. Mom and I understand."

And how well I understood. This child, who had the world at her feet and a full life ahead of her, was mourning the loss of the man who'd been her champion.

It was Zara who'd accused me of driving Andrew out of their lives when I packed them up and went to Aunt Celia's. It was Zara who'd insisted on sitting at the breakfast table next to her father every morning. It was Zara who'd once considered law school to please her dad.

And now it was Zara's heart being crushed by the loss.

Tears slid down my cheeks, and I brushed them away. "Zara, honey. We need to talk about your dad."

"What's there to talk about?" Zara continued to stare at her hands covered by Jonathan's.

"You're still missing him. And you will for a long, long time. He loved you very much." Needing to offer comfort, I stroked her shoulder.

"I wanted him to be here…when Andrew was born," she said just above a whisper, her voice shaking. "You can't imagine what it feels like to wake up after your child's born and know that your father will never see your baby."

I touched her cheek. "I wish I could do something."

She turned her tearstained face to me. "You can. Please, Mom. Please sell the house. Move somewhere safe, away from the memories so I don't have to worry about you."

Before I could react, she pulled her hands free and was up and out the door.

"I'll take her home, Mom. I'll be back later," Jonathan said, rising from his chair and following Zara.

I saw Jonathan drive carefully away, talking earnestly to his sister while Zara kept her head down.

And all I wanted to do was go out into the sunlight, away from the anguish stirring in me.

FEELING CONFUSED IN LIGHT of my children's attitude, I decided to weed the petunias. I was halfway across the yard to open the shed near the tree house when I spotted Sam coming toward me.

"I heard Zara sobbing when she got into the car. Did my kissing you upset her that much?" he asked, a look of concern on his face.

I blushed like a schoolgirl—and felt ridiculous. "The kids don't think I should be living here alone. They wanted to talk to me about selling the house."

And that kiss didn't help, I wanted to add, but I wasn't sure I could handle any discussion of our relationship or what it meant.

"Why would they want you to sell?"

"Lots of reasons in their minds," I said, feeling misunderstood by Zara and Jonathan. Yes, their concern was for my safety, but they didn't seem to grasp the important role this house had played in my life all these years, and how much I needed to keep things the way they were.

"Been there, done that—with Robert a few years ago."

"Really? What did you say to Robert?"

"That it was none of his damned business."

"You did?" I breathed.

"I did. He was irritated with me, but he got over it. And your children will, too."

"They'd better, or else." Brave words from a chicken-hearted woman, I mused to myself as I continued to watch this man who was rapidly becoming an essential part of my life.

"Just remember, whatever enters our lives, we can always dance," he said, gyrating as he grinned at me.

I laughed and suddenly felt much better—about everything.

CHAPTER TWELVE

JONATHAN RETURNED from taking Zara home in a much quieter mood. I asked him if he'd talked to Linda again, but he hadn't. He didn't say how he felt about being a father a second time over, which was sad. He loved children and should've been ecstatic.

When he said that he'd promised to go back and spend the evening with his sister while Gregory went into the office, I was relieved. I dreaded the idea that the two of them might want to argue with me over my staying in this house.

With the failing light making gold streaks across the length of my street, I decided to create a little baking mayhem in the form of the chocolate cake I'd promised Jonathan.

I pulled the flour from the lower cupboard, hearing the roar of Sam's lawn mower as he glided past the kitchen window. After having lunch with Sam the other day, I decided that I'd start having him for coffee whenever he mowed the lawn for me.

I'd invite Sam in when he'd finished. The chocolate cake was done and I was about halfway through a batch of chocolate-chip cookies when I heard a strange noise—a squeaky hinge sound.

Curious, I hurried down the hall toward the office, a chilly draft circling my legs.

I reached the door to the office and saw the window. "Who left it open?" I muttered, crossing the room, only to see a kid standing against the wall near Andrew's coin cabinet. My heart leaped into my throat. I stepped back.

"Don't make a move. I'm warning you," the kid said. Some part of my brain registered the fact that his voice was shaking.

"What are you doing here?" I asked, fighting the urge to run, while aware that any sudden move could be a mistake.

"What does it look like?" the kid demanded, glancing furtively toward the open window.

I swallowed. "It looks like you plan to steal from me."

The kid glared at me, his lips compressed into a hard line.

"Well, do you?" I asked.

"I was looking for money," he said sulkily, his glance swerving to the coin cabinet.

Oh, no, you don't, you little punk! Braver now, I moved closer, getting a better look at the intruder. This was just a kid—no more than thirteen would be my guess. "What's your name—"

A crash emanated from the hallway and Sam came roaring into the room, a shotgun in his hands and anger in his eyes.

"What's going on here?" he yelled, swinging the shotgun in a wide arc around the room.

"Sam! Don't!" I yelled.

The kid yelped as if in pain and vaulted out over the windowsill, hitting the flower bed outside with a muffled thud.

"You didn't shoot him, did you?" I asked in panic.

"Hell, no," Sam huffed, leaving his shotgun against the wall. "It wasn't loaded. I just wanted to frighten the little bastard."

"With a shotgun—"

"Which I've never fired in my life." He grinned, shamefaced.

"How did you know he was here?"

"I saw him go in the window."

"And you raced for your shotgun instead of the phone."

"You were alone."

"Should I feel better knowing that you went for a gun instead of the police?"

"Now that you mention it…"

Giving in to my relief that he was here, I hugged him, his solid body offering a shield from the past few minutes. Feeling the rapid rise and fall of his chest, I looked up at him. "Are you all right?"

He frowned at me, his eyes dark. "It's you I'm worried about."

"You came roaring in here ready to do battle. What if he'd been a real burglar?"

"He was, wasn't he?" Sam asked, still holding me.

"He was a kid who was more afraid than I was. He's probably home by now," I said, aware of Sam's arms.

His eyes glinted with humor. "You're telling me I look foolish."

"I've never been rescued like this. It's kind of nice."

"All I could think about when I saw him crawling through the window was that you were in here by yourself. If you'd been hurt…" He left the sentence unfinished and walked me out to the living room where he poured us each a large tumbler of Scotch.

He sat down on the sofa beside me, a look of concentration on his face. "This is probably not the appropriate time to say it, but I'm going to do it anyway."

"Say what?"

He took a long drink from his tumbler, stared at it and began. "Ever since Evelyn died, I've felt as if someone tore a chunk out of my heart. I'd always believed that I'd had my one chance at true love, that second chances didn't happen to men like me."

"Men like you?" I asked, feeling like a parrot.

"You know, what they call a nerd. A guy who reads Shakespeare, likes flowers, dresses oddly. I don't have charisma…"

Was Sam building up to some sort of confession?

I remembered him telling me I should find someone…that day in his kitchen. Hadn't he said he was looking for someone, too? Had he found her? And had I misunderstood his feelings?

Had I been wrong in harboring this idea that Sam and I might have more than a friendship?

And if I *was* wrong, why did I suddenly feel so sad?

"Do you believe you have a second chance at love, Emily?"

Was this Sam's way of telling me he did? Loneliness surrounded me as I spoke.

"Not really. I had my second chance when Andrew and I got back together," I said, feeling the old yearning for what would never be again.

I WAS SITTING IN THE LIVING room, thinking about Sam's intervention on my behalf, and his near-confession, when Jonathan arrived home from Zara's. I made myself sit still, acting all cool and in control when he joined me. "I'm glad you're home," I said, a funny squeakiness to my voice.

"Mom, you look like a ghost. What happened?"

I was past the "what do you mean" scene. Way past. "Someone broke in here tonight."

"What?" Jonathan stared at me. "Are you okay? Why didn't you call me?"

I never thought of it, wasn't the right answer. So I gave him the only excuse my addled brain could come up with. "He was just a kid, and he was as scared as I was."

"Did you call the police?"

Whoops. Didn't do that, either. "No. Sam got here and frightened the kid away. I didn't get a good look at him in the dark."

Jonathan sat down next to me on the sofa, in the exact place where Sam had recently sat. "Let me get this straight. Someone breaks in here, you don't call me, and Sam scares him off." He raked one hand through his hair. "Mom, Zara's right. This is no longer a safe neighborhood."

Oh God, my straight-as-an-arrow son is going to tell Warrior Zara. "Please don't worry her with this. She's got enough on her plate. I'm going to call a security company in the morning."

The slight frown of disapproval told me I needed to come up with a better answer. "Can we talk about this tomorrow? I'm very tired."

WITH EXHAUSTION—AND the very real possibility that I could've been hurt—making my limbs weak, I listened as Jonathan made his way through the house, checking the locks on every window and door.

"Okay, that's all we can do for tonight," he said from the top of the stairs.

"Thank you," I murmured, and meant it. I found it reassuring to have someone in the house with me. "I'm going to your father's office for a few minutes, then I'll be up."

"Night, Mom," he said as he gave me a weary smile.

As I walked slowly to Andrew's office, my mind cruised from one problem to another. Maybe my children were right. Maybe it wasn't a good idea to live alone in this big old house.

Flailed by the wind, the branches of the overgrown spirea snapped against the window, reminding me I needed to trim the shrubs and get the eaves troughs cleaned before winter.

Tired though I was, I didn't feel ready for sleep. I turned on the lamp and rooted around in the top drawer of the desk, looking for Andrew's address book. I had to get the fall chores done soon.

Loneliness swamped me as I lifted out Andrew's address book. There, in his neat handwriting, were pages of addresses of all the tradesmen I'd ever need. There were also notes written in the margins, along with instructions he'd left me for getting maintenance jobs done around the house.

Sitting alone in the dark looking for information on security systems, I was faced with the reality of what living here alone would be like.

How I wished I could talk to Andrew about getting a security system. If he were here, he'd go over the options, get the estimates and we'd have a system up and running in no time. Frantic to keep my anxious feelings from overwhelming me, I opened the bottom drawer, pulled out the letters and eased open the next one.

Dearest Emily,

I didn't get up this morning, and I could see the worry in your eyes. I'd like to reassure you that it won't happen again, but I can't. I can feel my body weakening. The simplest tasks, like shaving or brushing my teeth, take so much energy.

I made it down here to the office, but I'm exhausted by the effort. As each day passes, I feel the need to get the important stuff written down.

My mind floods with memories of our happy moments as you called them. Some of my best memories are those nights after we got back together and started talking to each other in the middle of the night again. How good it felt to hold you in my arms, to feel your warmth, your body folded into mine as we drifted off to sleep.

And even though we talk these days, there's such an urgency in what we say to each other. Reminiscing about our life together gets lost in the rush to talk about doctors' appointments, tests and how I'm feeling.

I cannot bring myself to share my emotional pain. I owe it to you to make this time as easy for you as possible, and there are no choices left for me, except to endure what's ahead.

As I watched you this morning doing your daily chores, I was reminded of something I should've said earlier in these letters. Emily, you're the most competent person I've ever known. You never ducked the work or the responsibility of keeping our lives running smoothly. It was you who kept our children safe and happy all these years.

I relied on you for so much. Whenever I had to make a decision about anything around this house, I could count on you to offer good advice. A part of me envied that sure-footed way you had of making decisions.

And that leads me to another point—the relief

I feel in knowing that you're able to cope without me. Oh, how it hurts to write those words!

There's no place I'd rather be than with you. How many times have I prayed for a miracle that would make me well. But I've come to accept that it will never be.

As I write this, I try to imagine how you'll feel as you read these letters. I started out believing that they were written to share my feelings, but now I realize these letters have given me an opportunity to encourage you to move on.

You have so much to look forward to as you face the future with our children and grandchildren. Our love made it possible for us to have a second chance. I want you to take pleasure in the everyday things of life, to know the joy of living each day. I want you to be happy, to find pleasure and love.

Life is yours to live. Please don't let it slip away.
Love always,
Andrew

I caressed the pages, my fingers tracing the lines, my pulse pounding. It was as if he were here in this room with me, as if he'd spoken the words he'd written. Until now I'd concentrated on what I'd lost when Andrew died, how lonely my life had become without him.

But he was still here in so many subtle ways: in how

I think, how I feel, and how I remember him. He's a part of everything that matters to me.

By what stroke of fate had I read this letter at this moment, just when I needed a boost in self-confidence? Reading his words of praise and understanding have helped more than he could ever have imagined when he wrote them.

LATE THE NEXT MORNING I perched on the wicker sofa in the screened-in porch. After reading Andrew's letter last night, I slept in our old bedroom, something I hadn't been able to do in all these months. It held too many memories of nights together.

The memories of Andrew's last hours in that bedroom were playing through my mind when Sam appeared with his paper and his coffee. When I saw him framed in the door, my stomach did a strange jig.

"How come you're up so early?" he asked, opening the door to the porch.

"I have lots to do," I replied as he moved to his usual chair, where he'd sat so many evenings with Andrew.

"We're going dancing tonight, aren't we?"

I'd forgotten. "Yes, we are."

As I watched him set his cup down on the wicker table, I was surprised at how perfectly normal it felt to be sitting here talking with Sam.

Sam rubbed his jaw, took a sip of coffee and glanced my way. "I want to talk to you about getting a dusk-to-dawn light in our backyards. It would help discourage the kids from coming through here from the ravine. I've entertained the idea of getting a couple of trees cut down in the back to make it harder for them to hide, but I hate to destroy something so beautiful. What do you think?"

"I think a light's an excellent idea, especially after last night."

A part of me felt good about Sam's actions last night. Who else would have rushed to my defense? I let my gaze move over his face, across the frown lines between his eyes, the set of his jaw, the brooding blue of his eyes, all the familiar features. "Thank you for being there."

"You're welcome."

Seeing how comfortably he sat beside me, making me feel a part of his world, I realized this could become a very pleasant morning ritual. And if it did? Were we destined to have a friendship as close as he'd had with my husband?

"Now, about the dance classes…"

I was listening to him describe how the one class he'd attended on his own had been populated by klutzes and dance divas—when Jonathan entered the porch.

"Hi, Mom, and thanks for the chocolate cake. It made a great breakfast." He grinned and kissed my forehead and sat down next to me. "Nice to see you, Sam," he said, shaking Sam's hand before searching my eyes.

"You mother's agreed we should get a light in the yard to ward off intruders."

"Sounds like a step in the right direction. Mom also needs to upgrade the security inside the house. But I'm not sure that a light in the backyard is enough protection."

"What would you suggest?" Sam asked.

"Mom should consider moving to a condo or an apartment where there's more protection for a woman living alone."

"She's not alone here. She has neighbors."

I was proud of the hint of indignation in Sam's voice, and very pleased to have his support.

Jonathan's back stiffened. "But she's still alone in the house, and after last night, we need to help her make other living arrangements."

Wait a minute. I'm not having my morning coffee ruined by an argument. "We'll talk about this later, Jonathan." I patted his hand and gave him my no-more-about-this look.

"Your mother's agreed to go ballroom dancing with me," Sam said, his tone definitely on the bragging side.

Jonathan sent me a measured look. "That sounds like fun."

Was that his code phrase for disapproval? "I decided it's time for me to find myself, as Zara's so fond of saying," I responded.

Jonathan smiled. "That's great, Mom."

So he didn't object to my plans for ballroom dance classes. I didn't want Jonathan to be upset with me. "I plan to get out and enjoy myself, live a little."

"I'm glad to hear that. Zara will be, too." Jonathan

glanced at his watch. "I need to pack and get to the airport."

His eyes told me he wanted me with him. "I'll come and help you," I said.

IN THE QUIET OF THE living room, Jonathan and I faced each other. "I wish you could stay longer."

"Me, too, Mom. But I have to get home. And this time away, talking to you and Zara, has helped me think more clearly. I've got to deal with what's going on between Linda and me."

I tucked a check between his fingers. "I want to pay for your rental car."

"You don't have to do that," he protested.

"Your father would've done this, and he would've supported you in any way he could. Your happiness meant everything to him."

I wanted to tell my son once again to take things slow, to see how he and Linda really felt about each other, but I couldn't bring myself to say anything. As much as I felt the urge to start offering more advice, I didn't want my son to feel pressured by my expectations.

"Be good to yourself, and I'm here if you need me. Any hour of the day or night," I whispered, remembering my call to him a few days ago.

"I'll phone when I get home. Will you be all right?"

Oh, dear son of mine, be happy and safe and loved.

"Sure. I've got lots to do. Kate and I are going out to lunch. Then there's dance class." I winked at him.

"I can't believe this. You're finally going dancing. I wonder when Sam decided to take it up?"

"He says he's always wanted to learn to dance."

"Really? He and Dad used to joke about how neither of them could tell one foot from the other. He's putting the moves on you, Mom."

I forced myself to grin. "Don't be silly. Sam? I suspect he already has a woman. Besides, he's not my type."

"Says who?"

"Your mother. Now get on the road, and call me once you're home," I said, to cover an odd feeling of sadness, the same one I'd felt last night.

"If I were Sam, *I'd* be putting the moves on you."

"You're not, and he isn't, so let's forget it." We hugged each other goodbye. We stood together as we'd done so many times before. Each time I kidded myself into believing that it was easier to see him off, back to his own life, but it wasn't, and it never would be.

From the end of the driveway, I watched the brake lights on Jonathan's car as he turned right onto Hudson and out of sight.

CHAPTER THIRTEEN

FEELING ABSOLUTELY STUFFED from lunch with Kate, I sat down in Andrew's chair to read another letter, glancing around to be sure I'd left nothing out of place after the incident a night ago. I braced myself for the all-too-familiar ache of loneliness, the tears at the unfairness of it all. Those feelings were still there but not nearly as bad as before. It was more a sense of yearning now, tempered by acceptance.

It'd been ten days since I started reading these letters from Andrew, and during those days I'd come to see how comforting his words were. His letters had given me a chance to see our life through his eyes.

Fergus bunted his head against my leg. "Want up, big guy?" I asked, reaching down and lifting him onto my lap. "Fergus, I'm getting you a treadmill for Christmas," I scolded as he snuggled his ample body close to mine, and I opened the letter.

Dearest Emily,
May 21, one more month until summer's underway. You've been fussing in the vegetable

garden all morning, trying to coax the lettuce to grow big enough to be part of a salad.

As I sit here looking out on the backyard, I'm reminded of that wonderful Saturday morning in early May three years ago, just after Megan was born, when you planted your climbing rose in front of the trellis next to the porch. I watched you, enjoying the methodical way you worked.

When you looked up and saw me, you smiled from under your broad-brimmed straw hat. The love in your eyes made me want to cling to the moment the way a shipwreck victim would cling to a life raft. It was as if everything in our lives had led to that moment—our marriage, our life together and the arrival of our first grandchild.

I waved and you waved back before getting up and coming to the kitchen window. I opened the window and you grinned up at me, offering me a chance to earn my keep by working for you. Seeing you so happy, I tossed aside the journal I was reading and came outside. As I sat on the porch and listened to your commentary about the garden and your plans for it, I felt a rush of longing for all the missed moments we didn't share because of my work.

Later that day, the scent of honeysuckle hovered over us as we ate our lunch of Caesar salad and chicken, washed down with a glass of Chardonnay. That day is one of my very best memories.

Today, I try to nap but can't. I managed to gather enough energy to come back in here to my desk. Still, tired though I feel, my mind can't seem to stop remembering....

How much we enjoyed playing with Megan— and the weekend she spent with us before Jonathan and Linda moved to Seattle. I can still see you holding baby Megan in your arms, dancing around the room as you sang to her, a smile on your face, despite the fact that Megan, Jonathan and Linda would be on their way in a few hours.

And the day Zara and Gregory were married in our backyard. I remember how hard you worked to have the gardens just perfect, and the way she looked at us that afternoon, as if seeing us for the first time. A wonderful girl, through and through.

Yet the most wonderful woman in my life will always be you.

As I sit here, trying to prepare for what is ahead, I can't help wondering about my in-credible good fortune that you were in the library that particular day. So many events in our separate lives led up to it, ensuring that we were both in the library at that moment.

As I write these words, I feel my hand begin to shake, the ever-present exhaustion clawing at me like some relentless beast.

How I wish I could make love the way we

*used to, but I can't, and it shames me more than
I could ever have imagined.*

*And now, as the light begins to fade from under
the trees along the back of the property, and the
wind has eased to a whisper, I'm reminded of just
how lucky I've been in my life. I've known the best
of times, and now I'm to experience the worst of
times.*

*None of it matters, as long as you're here
with me and I'm with you.*

*I'm not a religious man, but I do believe you
and I were destined to be together.*
Love always,
Andrew

I bit my lip to hold back the tears. I remembered that
day so well. Andrew had been getting steadily weaker.
The gray pallor of his skin, his breathing difficulties
and his restlessness terrified me. Digging in the earth
was my salvation.

Remembering that time reminded me of another. It
was late one night, two weeks before he had to be
admitted to hospital….

Lying still so as not to disturb his restless sleep,
I listen for his raspy breathing. Jonathan arrived
today. His presence in the house brings a frail smile
to Andrew's lips.

Tears seep through my lashes but I no longer
care how many tears I cry. My heart pounds with

love for the man lying beside me in our bed, his body a dim replica of its former self.

Feeling a cramp start in my foot, I flex my toes.

"Are you awake?" Andrew asks.

"I'm sorry, I didn't mean to disturb you," I whisper, turning to face him in the darkness.

"I wasn't asleep. I was lying here, trying not to wake you."

"We're a strange pair," I say, taking his bony hand in mine.

"We are." He squeezes my fingers, and I can't stop myself from thinking that this could be our last night in this bed. I can't free my mind of the fear that we're having our last days together. Andrew goes to his oncologist today, and he'll be going in a wheelchair. I smother a sob and force my thoughts to something positive. "Connor called after you went to bed last night," I tell him.

"He did?"

The listlessness in Andrew's voice frightens me. "Yes. He's coming home on Tuesday."

"I'm glad…so glad. I want you to have the children with you when I go into the hospital."

"Andrew, don't say that. I don't want—"

"We have to talk." He shifts closer to me. "We probably won't have another opportunity, and there are so many feelings, so many memories, I can't keep them straight."

"You don't have to. We're going to take care of you."

"Emily, listen to me. Life is what you make it. It's how we deal with a problem, not the problem itself, that tests us."

What's he saying? Does he know something he's not telling me? Did something happen in the night? I fight the rising panic. "I don't *want* to be tested."

"You've always faced our problems better than I have over the years, and you have to continue."

I can't tell him I don't want to face anything ever again. I'm petrified when I imagine my life without him. "Let's not talk about this."

"Promise me something."

"Anything," I manage to say, panic rearing up in me.

"Promise me you'll remember every moment we spent together, and you'll share those memories with our children. Then, let the memories go and make room for a new life."

"I…no, this isn't right."

"Emily, right or wrong, that's the way it is." He moves my hands to his lips and kisses my fingers. We cuddle together, the sound of his labored breathing invading the stillness.

Looking back now, I realize that moment was one that will be forever engraved on my heart. I felt closer to Andrew than at any other time in our lives.

An hour later, after I'd scrubbed the kitchen floor on my hands and knees, I had finally forced the memories out of my mind. I was giving serious consideration to cleaning the freezer when a loud banging on the back door startled me.

Nearly slipping on the freshly scrubbed tiles, I peered through the glass panels. It was Sam, and he looked as if someone had torn up his precious rose garden. "What's up?" I asked, opening the door. "Is dance class canceled?"

"No, I need to talk to you."

I'd never seen him so agitated. "Come in."

He seemed to burst in the door. "I can't stay. I have hours of work to do outside. Are you still interested in helping Phillip?"

"Sure. When do you want me to start?"

"Is today too soon?"

"It's that urgent?" I asked, trying not to be too obvious in my perusal of Sam. His eyes were red rimmed and dark. He hadn't shaved.

"Phillip's teacher is very unhappy with his reading abilities. She says he should've done remedial reading this summer. You were right all along. He needs to be assessed for his learning abilities, but I can't seem to get that message across to my son and his ex-wife. If you could work with him on his reading while I work on the parents…"

Between my concern for Zara and my promise to get Andrew's office cleaned out, not to mention wanting to visit with my grandson, Sam's request came at an awkward time. But the pleading in Sam's eyes made me want to help. "What about early next week?"

"That would be wonderful. I really appreciate this. I don't want Phillip to have more problems than he already has."

He was referring to Robert's ditzy ex-wife, I was pretty sure. It was Andrew who labeled her ditzy after many hours of listening to Sam describe the outrageous escapades of his daughter-in-law. "I'll see what I can do."

"Thanks." He took my hands between his huge ones, his skin surprisingly warm. He leaned down to give me a quick kiss. "About the class tonight, does seven sound okay?"

Next time you kiss me, I want a little warning so I can join in. Or maybe I wasn't meant to. Maybe Sam's kiss was in friendship only…. "Seven will be fine."

"I'll pick you up. What would you say to having coffee after our class."

A date? "Coffee would be nice," I said, wondering what was really going on behind those expressive blue eyes.

I smoothed my hair and fluffed my bangs as I watched him skip down my back steps and stride across to his own property.

THE RESTROOM AT THE dance class needed a coat of paint and an interior decorator. It was nearly time for the class to start, and I desperately wanted a few moments alone.

"Why did I agree to do this?" I asked my image in the mirror—then cringed at the thought that someone might be in one of the cubicles.

Sam and I had driven downtown to the dance class in stark silence. I couldn't have come up with a topic of conversation to save my soul and obviously neither could he. He spent the twenty minutes in the car frowning and gripping the wheel as if it was trying to get away from him.

And now he was waiting for me on the dance floor, and I had the overpowering urge to climb out the window and hail a cab.

The night would not end well. Of that I was certain.

What would we say to each other? We exchanged our bleak comments about the weather when I first got into his Subaru station wagon, just ahead of the verbal blackout. Wishing I could develop a sudden attack of some highly contagious—but not serious—disease and have to be rushed home, I checked my makeup and adjusted the neckline of my dress.

What made me think this was a good idea? Seeing nothing in the mirror that would explain my temporary insanity, I rubbed my sweaty palms together and left the ladies' room.

When I reached the dance floor, Sam was there—his long, lanky body draped along the far wall. The incandescent light in the large room softened his craggy features. When he smiled at me, I managed to smile back.

I glanced around, looking for another couple our age, but all I saw were young men with their hip-jutting poses and the wide, flirtatious smiles of their young partners. Feeling frumpy and keenly aware of my thickening waist, I kept my eyes on Sam. His smile was encouraging, and the way he pushed off from the wall was pure James Dean.

I hadn't worn a dress and heels in ages, so the feel of the smooth cotton swinging around my legs as I teetered across the floor was oddly exhilarating. Sam watched me, and I was unnerved by the awareness in his eyes.

Stop it! This is your neighbor—your somewhat odd neighbor whose poodle watches you from the living room window.

"Are you ready?" he asked, holding out his hand as I drew near.

"Why not?" I replied, focusing on what lay ahead.

We stood there staring at each other as the seconds ticked past. Finally, the instructor pranced onto the center of the floor, flicking a glance our way, a gleam of disapproval in his eyes. His pompous arrival gave us something other than our mutual discomfort to focus on.

Eddy St. Simon was one of those thin-nosed, thin-bodied people who you suspected from the stiff set of his mouth would be one royal pain in the butt. He did not disappoint.

He herded us all out on the floor with phony words of encouragement mixed in with orders to stand straight, face your partner, heads up, smile. I fantasized about stomping out.

He worked his way among the couples, offering smiles to some, frowns of haughty displeasure to others, reaching Sam and me last. With an exaggerated sigh, he picked up our arms and moved them into position, making a funny sucking sound with his lips. He finally had Sam and me aligned to his satisfaction. The music began—a Tommy Dorsey tune.

Sam tightened his arm around me and gently squeezed my hand. We stood so close I could feel the heat of his body and the fresh lavender scent of his cotton shirt. I rested my hand on his shoulder.

Eddy took my hand, pulled it farther up Sam's shoulder and hissed in my ear, "Hold your wrist as if you're looking at your watch." He gave my wrist a not-so-gentle twist and roared off to the next couple.

Sam and I were left alone to follow the caller who was carefully enunciating each dance move. "I feel it's only fair to warn you that I like to lead," I told him.

"That's what happens when you dance alone in your living room at night," Sam said, chuckling as he pulled me closer.

"Just keep it in mind, that's all I ask."

"As long as you don't forget who's watching our moves. You wouldn't want to upset you-know-who," Sam said, taking a daring step toward me. I took an equally daring step toward him. We collided in the middle. Trying to regain our balance, he grabbed my waist, and I felt myself swooping toward the hardwood floor as I locked my fingers onto his shirt.

So much for watching my watch.

"Did the commander see us?" Sam asked. He tugged me upright and I landed on his feet rag-doll style.

"Do we care?" I squeezed out the words as I sneaked a peek in Eddy's direction. The man had some unfortunate couple cornered on the other side of the room. We did our best to concentrate on our feet while making a stab at shuffling in time with the music.

"I'm getting the hang of this," Sam said jovially as he planted one of his big feet firmly on my arch. I wanted to howl with pain, but checked it when I saw the embarrassed look on his face.

"They have a mind of their own," he murmured by way of explanation, looking first at his feet and then at me.

"They sure do." My foot burned with pain.

"Okay, dancers, let's move to the music," ordered Eddy St. Simon, appearing out of nowhere, his creepy hands landing on my waist. "This is the correct position," he admonished, lifting Sam's arm farther up my back.

Eddy stepped back and checked us over with the expression of someone who'd just smelled something rotten. "Now, little lady, let's see you hold your wrist properly. Maybe the two of you should consider taking private lessons. I'm available," Eddy said.

I was about a breath away from indulging in some really childish actions, like sticking out my tongue. Then I glanced up at Sam and saw the scowl on his face as he grimly tried to keep his feet moving in the right order.

"Now, you two continue practicing and I'll be back."

I felt Sam's arm tighten on me as he disentangled

his feet from between mine for about the tenth time. "Should we take him up on his offer of private lessons?" he asked.

"Not in this lifetime."

"I wonder if we might be smarter to work at this on our own."

"Sam Bannister, what are you suggesting?"

"I've seen the way you dance. It's so much smoother than what we're doing here."

Was that a compliment? His words seemed sincere. "That's kind of you to say."

"I'm not being kind, I mean it."

We stumbled along for a few more minutes, our knees bumping occasionally as we clutched each other. "What are we doing here?" Sam gasped in dismay after a particularly clumsy collision.

"Learning to dance?"

Eddy glowered at us from the other side of the room. I could see that he was torn between working with the agile couple in front of him, or coming across the room and propping us up yet again.

Sam held me tighter, stopped moving his feet and whispered, "Do we need him in our lives?"

He was reading my mind. "We definitely do not. Want to make a getaway?" I asked in my best conspirator's voice.

"Sounds like a plan to me. We'd better make our move before he sees us standing still. I don't want another lecture."

"Then let's dance our way out of here. You lead."

We danced somewhat awkwardly toward the exit, chuckling like a pair of schoolkids. "Think he saw us?" I asked as I wobbled on my heels into the parking lot with Sam's arm steadying me.

"I don't care if he did," Sam said triumphantly, pulling me against him and hugging the air out of my lungs.

I tilted my chin and smiled up at him, at this man who was willing to risk looking foolish. "I don't care, either."

"Why don't we dance out here in the parking lot?" he asked, doing his version of a slow waltz over the asphalt.

Not bad. "You're making real progress," I declared, trying to keep the surprise from my voice.

"Just call me Fred," he said with a smirk.

"Astaire, that is?"

He nodded. "And you'd be?"

"Ginger Rogers, of course." And I did a little dance step all my own.

He twirled me around once and let me go. I danced across the lot, moving to imaginary music. Halfway to the car I heard clapping.

"That's wonderful. But then, you've had practice." Sam followed me across the lot, taking my hand in his as if he'd done it a thousand times before.

"And you've been peeking in my windows," I said, enjoying the way he looked at me, the easy way we shared our thoughts.

"Do you blame me?" He drew me toward him.

In his eyes I saw challenge mingled with affection. The air stilled between us as his eyes swept over my face. "Emily, you're one hell of a woman."

Was he flirting with me? I was so out of practice I couldn't be sure. And if he was, why couldn't I come up with something clever and sophisticated to say? I was standing in a parking lot with a—yes—handsome man on a beautiful evening. A man who was my neighbor, my friend and someone who understood what I'd been through.

If I could string a couple of sentences together, what would I want to say? That being here with him like this was one of those crazy moments between two people? That the vulnerable look in his eyes was too real for me right now? Or did I simply lack the social skills to deal with a man who was trying to pay me a compliment?

Before I could respond, Sam asked, "Would you like to go for coffee?" His voice was tentative as he opened the car door for me.

I climbed into the seat and he went around to the driver's side and slid in. I couldn't look at him, not with so many feelings roaring through me. I felt light-hearted, excited, bursting with hope for the future. And most of all, I felt the warmth of Sam's physical presence. And it felt…right.

"I make the best espresso on the planet," Sam said as he started the car and pulled out of the parking lot.

"You're inviting me to your house," I said stupidly.

"Yeah, that's the plan." He glanced my way. "Don't look so scared."

I smoothed my expression into what I hoped was one of pleasant interest. "Me? Scared? Hardly."

My real fear was that this was all progressing too quickly.

While I plucked my imaginary worry beads, Sam drove to his house, parked the car and, with gallantry and charm, escorted me into his living room—which had a great view of my living room windows. While we chatted he made the best cup of espresso I'd ever had.

Sitting on the sofa next to him, sipping my coffee, I realized how enjoyable the evening had been despite the dance instructor's behavior. Sitting here with Sam, chatting like old friends was the perfect end to the day. "Thanks, Sam."

"For what?"

"The evening. Your espresso. Out of curiosity, who told you I liked espresso?" He raised his eyebrows at me. "Cancel that." I already knew the answer.

Sam ran his fingers over the back of the sofa, nearly touching my shoulder. I was surprised to discover that I *wanted* him to touch me and kiss me the way he'd done before.

"Andrew and I sometimes talked about you, even before he got sick. You see, I loved the subject," Sam said.

"Me?" I stared at Sam, the man who'd paid me only the slightest interest, who always seemed preoccupied when he talked to me.

"Andrew and I would talk about you occasionally, usually about something you said or did. But when you and Andrew were separated, he talked about you a lot more. At first I tried not to take it in. It was too hard for me. But Andrew was my best friend, and it was very difficult to watch him go through so much pain and misery."

My heart went out to Sam. "You were very good to him, and in one of his letters he mentioned that he was glad you were there to help him get his life back."

"My motives were not just those of a friend. I was half in love with you and secretly hoped your marriage *was* over—so I'd have a chance. But the anguish in Andrew's eyes told me he wasn't over you, and he would never be…and that made two of us."

My head felt light and funny. Sam was watching me carefully, as if I'd just landed from Mars. "You're…in love with me? But you were Andrew's friend. You hardly gave me the time of day. You didn't even seem to like me."

Sam eased me into his arms, and without any pretense or warning, he kissed me. The kind of kiss that made me want to head straight to his bedroom.

He released me, taking my hands in his. "It was a bit of a precarious situation. I was in love with a woman who was in love with my best friend. I didn't stand a chance."

My heart literally skipped a beat.

CHAPTER FOURTEEN

SAM WILL PROBABLY never speak to me again.

After he kissed me, I all but catapulted out of his house, through the backyard and home.

Sam Bannister loved me.

Now I had to figure out what to do about it. We couldn't live side by side—having almost daily contact—without some sort of understanding.

I'd been up since six, emptied the dishwasher, repotted four houseplants and fed Fergus far too much food. All because I woke early this morning and couldn't get back to sleep. For the first time since Andrew's death, I didn't wake from the usual dream that he was calling to me. I simply opened my eyes.

Was this how it would happen? I'd start to enjoy myself, fill my life with people and places and spend less and less time thinking about Andrew? Would I begin to forget the sound of his laughter, his wonderful enthusiasm, the way he kissed me?

Yet deep inside I was well aware that my night had been different because of Sam and his profession of love.

Sam was kind, thoughtful, funny, protective—and he could kiss.

I, on the other hand, didn't have a clue what I felt or wanted—except maybe to be held and kissed and…

Feeling guilty about those feelings, I sat at Andrew's desk and looked around the room at the things that had made up Andrew's life.

I took a photo of Andrew from the credenza behind his desk and studied it, reminiscing about the day the photo had been taken. A local photographer covering the story of one of Andrew's trials took the shot and published it in the paper. I contacted the photographer and had the photo framed for Andrew's fiftieth birthday party. We had so much to celebrate that particular birthday. Connor was finally through all of his recon-struction surgeries, Zara loved her education degree program and Jonathan had begun his career as an ar-chitect.

And now with his last letter to read, was this the end of a journey for me? I touched the mahogany photo frame as I had so many mornings in the past months—only today I felt different. Changed somehow.

I reached into the drawer and pulled out the letters with the realization that I would miss this morning ritual. Needing to feel Andrew's presence, I tore open the envelope with the number eleven in the right-hand corner.

Dearest Emily,
The heat of July is upon us, but I don't feel it.
We can no longer hide what this disease is
doing to us, to our remaining time together. I'm

too sick to stay at my desk, and I can't face seeing my office knowing that I'll never practice law again.

As I sit here, I listen for the sound of you, memorizing the moment, while I wonder how and when you'll find these letters.

There's very little time left to consider what our life would have been had I not developed this horrible illness, but if there's one thing I need to do, it's help you see how much you have to offer the people you love and care for, and I'm not talking only about our family.

Emily, you must come to terms with the idea that your life will go on without me. We've experienced so much together, loved each other through thick and thin, learned from each other—and now I have to make one final plea.

Find happiness. Take your life back and let me go. You need to find joy, to experience all that is beautiful in this world. The thought of you living alone without someone to cherish breaks my heart. You have to be open to what will happen next. Please promise me that you'll let love into your life again.

I love you. I'll always love you. Nothing will ever change that. You and I will be together, connected and part of each other, for all eternity.
Love always,
Andrew

My chest hurt; my sobs scared Fergus off his usual perch on my lap. This was unfair, so damned unfair. I swiped at the tears and glanced around, looking for anything to distract me. But everything in this room reminded me of Andrew.

Oh, how much I'd like to talk to him, to hear his voice one last time. To ask him about so many things that seemed insignificant back then, but now seem so vital.

As I stared through my tears at his letter, I was struck by a possibility. I dug around in the desk drawer and retrieved a pen, reached into the bottom drawer and pulled out one of the same vellum sheets he'd used.

> *My darling Andrew,*
> *There is not a day that I don't think about you, about what you said, how you felt, what I did or didn't do. Or how we managed to survive those last months without one of us going crazy. And that would most certainly have been me! Not you. Never you.*
>
> *When I first found your letters, I didn't know if I wanted to read them, or how I'd feel being privy to your thoughts. Yet, with each letter, I'm becoming less afraid of my life, and more in control of the future. Your letters have been my salvation.*
>
> *From the moment you told me about the diagnosis I lived in fear of the end and what it*

would be like. I wanted you at home with me for as long as possible. I got my wish. Those last days were so blessed. It was as if we were communicating telepathically. I was in your head and you in mine. When your time came, I felt as if you were being torn from me.

It takes my breath away to realize that even as you were facing the end of your life, your only concern was for my welfare. How could you be so unselfish? How could your last thoughts be of me?

My darling, one thing I am certain of in this world—you and I were meant to be. I promise you, I'm not going to dwell on the past the way I've been doing. I know I've worried my children and my friends but I'm going to move forward.

I'm going to remember the good times we had, the fun, the love and the way we lived for each other. That's the best anyone could ask for.

And my love, I've had the best. Wherever my life leads me now can never compare to our life with each other.
Love always,
Emily

Zara's voice interrupted me as I read over my letter, and I was glad. Not that I didn't mean every word I'd written, but I was emotionally exhausted. "I'm in here, in your father's office," I called, getting out of the chair and hurrying down the hall to the kitchen.

Zara was standing in the entrance, and little Andrew's car seat was in the middle of the table. She had a strange look on her face. "Mom, I am so upset. Why didn't you tell me about the break-in?"

I stopped, trying to find a reason why I hadn't told her. The truth was I didn't want a lecture about the dangers of living alone, but I couldn't tell her that.

"I guess it slipped my mind. I assumed Jonathan would tell you."

"Thankfully, he did." Zara peered around as if looking for something.

"Want a cup of tea?" I started for the stove and the teakettle.

Andrew whimpered and squirmed in his car seat, and we both reached for him, our hands brushing.

I squeezed my daughter's fingers. "Zara, please don't be upset about this. You're not responsible for me. I've told you that a dozen times."

"Are you going to sell this house?"

"No, Zara, I can't do that."

"Why not?"

I wanted to wrap my arms around her, but the accusation in her voice stopped me. "Zara, I'm going to stay in this house. I have to, and not just because I miss your father. I want to keep our things."

Zara rolled her eyes. "Yeah, I realize that—but why?"

"There was a lot of love in my family when I was growing up, but that's about all there was. We had nothing, and my father worked hard for us to have even the basics. My parents made huge sacrifices to send me to college. I grew up not wanting to part with anything that might prove useful. As the years went by, keeping things gave me such pleasure, such a sense of security, I couldn't let them go."

"You're talking about the Thunderbird, right?" Zara said, frowning.

"The Thunderbird, the attic full of toys, the grandfather clock my uncle gave me and, of course, this house." I glanced around the kitchen, taking in the decorative plates on the wall above the cabinets and the open cupboard stacked with china dishes. "I need to stay connected with the past."

Zara slid into the chair beside me. "Is that why you're hanging on to Dad?"

"He and I were a part of each other's lives for so many years. In his letters, he's been telling me how he felt about the life we shared. I read the last letter just a little while ago. Zara, your father and I had a wonderful marriage."

The ticking of the wall clock filled the room as I waited for Zara to speak. I could handle anything from her but silence.

"I envy you… I wish he'd written to me." Her voice shook so badly I could hardly understand her words. "I wish for so many things." Her eyes shifted to Andrew, who was now sleeping peacefully in his car seat.

I watched as she rested her elbows on the table and her chin on her hands—an endearing action, one she'd done all her life.

"Mom, I don't know how to tell you this."

"You can tell me anything," I said, relieved she was ready to talk.

"Gregory's boss wants him to accept another position in Atlanta. This time it's a huge promotion. If he doesn't take it, he won't be offered another promotion for a very long time. If ever."

My daughter and her family in Atlanta.

I gulped air to keep from crying out. How would I live without her? I needed Zara with me, now more than ever. Surely my son-in-law could find a job closer than Atlanta! He'd turned down other jobs and it hadn't ended his career.

"Mom, say something."

I wanted to beg her not to leave, to be with me the way she'd always been from the day she was born— not only my daughter, but my friend, my lifeline. I felt the impending loss of her like a physical force that threatened to shred my world into a million pieces. "When would you move?" I asked through dry lips.

"Gregory has to be in Atlanta by the end of November."

A few weeks away. Oh God, I can't do this. It's too soon. There's so much we still have to straighten out. And how will she cope alone with a new baby without her mother close by?

My arms trembled from the urge to pull her into my embrace and plead with her not to go, to promise me that she'd stay and allow me to keep some part of my life the way it had always been.

I looked into her face and saw the hesitation in her eyes, and I knew in that instant that I had to be strong for her. She needed to hear me say that leaving was all right, that I was happy for her and Gregory and Andrew. My gaze swerved to the precious infant asleep between us, while my mind leaped to Andrew and what he'd say if he was here.

It was in this moment of terrible reckoning that it hit me. I was no longer part of a whole, a couple. I had to face the situation on my own.

What am I going to say?

I searched her face for the answer. What I saw was my little girl—the same little girl who solved everything in her brothers' lives. And recently, despite everything that had been going on in her own life, she was the woman who'd been working diligently on fixing mine.

But now she needed *me* to fix something for *her.* She needed me to understand that she had to move, for her husband's sake and for her family. She had to make a home for the people she loved.

Her need for my approval shone in her eyes. And beyond that, I saw that she had to know I'd be all right without her. I took a deep breath. "I've heard wonderful things about Atlanta. Huge city, lots going on. You'll love living there."

The tension in Zara's face slipped away. She crushed me in a sweeping hug that nearly landed me on the floor. "Oh, Mom! I'm so glad to hear you say that."

I patted her back and remembered my life at her age. Andrew and I figured we could handle anything, go anywhere.

And in so many ways we did.

"Love you, pet. And give Gregory my congratulations."

"Thanks, Mom. And you'll come to visit us in Atlanta soon…please."

Somehow I'd managed to say the words my daughter desperately needed to hear. I touched her cheek and she turned her face into my hand the way she used to do as a child. "You bet," I murmured. "Wild horses couldn't keep me away."

We probably would've sat there hugging each other for a while longer if Andrew hadn't started to howl. Zara laughed and reached for the straps holding her son secure in his seat.

I sat back in my chair and watched, my heart in my throat, as my daughter picked up her baby and cradled him against her. I was reminded of moments like this in my own life—me holding Zara in my arms, the two of us tucked away in our own private world.

"Mom, there's something else."

I didn't want to hear one more thing today, but when my daughter and her family left for Atlanta, there wouldn't be a chance to sit here like this and listen to her thoughts. Sure, we'd have the phone. But the phone wouldn't be able to tell me what her expression was, or how wide her smile. "More news?"

"Gregory and I had a long talk when he came home

to tell me about Atlanta. We talked about our future, and what life would be like in Atlanta and…and it dawned on me what I've done to you. Unintentionally. I've let you think Gregory and I have been staying here because of you and what you've been going through.

"The truth is, I couldn't bring myself to leave. After Dad died, I couldn't see myself living anywhere but here, close to home. I couldn't bear to go because I felt I wouldn't just be leaving you, but Dad, as well."

"Maybe you were missing your father much more than you realized. Maybe you were being strong for me. That's one of your best traits."

Zara and I looked at each other and I saw her father in the way her eyes searched mine.

"Gregory and I talked about Dad the other night. He made me see that I wasn't coping well with Dad's death. He convinced me that it might help to get away from the memories. And he promised me that if I'm not happy in Atlanta, he'll find a job in this area."

Wonders never cease. "Gregory's a good husband."

Zara raised Andrew to her shoulder and gently rubbed his tiny back. "It's so weird, Mom. I was in love with Gregory when I married him, but you know what?"

I had a pretty good idea what was coming next. "What?"

"I've never loved him more than when he made me that promise."

CHAPTER FIFTEEN

IT'S OCTOBER 23, A day of mixed emotions. I'd just had a call from Barry and Sheila Snow, the best man and maid of honor at our wedding. They'd called from Tampa to see how I was doing on what would have been my fortieth wedding anniversary, a day I'd been dreading for months.

And I might still have dreaded it, if not for Andrew's letters.

It made me sad not to have any more of his letters. I'd gotten accustomed to reading his thoughts. Over our nearly forty years of marriage, we'd learned to communicate in a kind of short-hand, predicting what the other would say, finishing each other's sentences.

It wasn't that we took each other for granted, although I guess we did at times, but rather that we'd grown close enough to see the pattern of our life together. He never failed to recognize the signs of an impending, impassioned discussion on changes to school policy, my special interest. And I'd learned to understand that his long hours of pacing his office was his way of working off the frustration of losing a case.

These varied parts of our lives added up, over time, to two people who knew each other intimately at all levels. This intimacy was what allowed us to share the burden of Andrew's illness.

As I looked ahead to today, I decided not to give Andrew's letters to our children. They were between Andrew and me, my last intimate connection to my husband.

What I could share, I decided as I spread boiled icing on the chocolate cake, was Andrew's wish that I move on. My children wanted me to find a new life, and they'd offered their support by agreeing to be here today to celebrate my anniversary.

Feeling a need for one last look at the letters before my family arrived, I quickly finished icing the cake.

Back in his office, I pulled open the drawer and took them out.

They were letters of love, and of faith in who we were as a couple. What we meant to each other. I fought back the sense of panic rushing through me as I recognized anew that I'd never see my husband again.

But I wasn't alone. I had my friends. I had our children and our grandchildren to remind me that life goes on, that life was for those willing to live it. I had so much to be thankful for.

And then there was Sam, and the butterflies in my stomach when I thought of him. Sweet, endearing Sam…

I was staring into space when I heard a car in the driveway. Minutes later, Connor's voice boomed in the front hall.

"Hey, Mom! Where are you?" I heard his cane clomp on the wood floor in rhythm with his words.

"I'm in here." I charged down the hall, holding out my arms. "You're late."

"And you're lucky I could get a flight on such short notice."

Knowing how awkward it was for Connor to sit confined in economy, I'd bought him a business-class ticket. "Tell me how everything went."

"I had a great flight, sat next to a truly wonderful woman. An artist. She paints huge murals and loves sixties music."

Could my son have found someone special? "You like her?"

"Hold your matchmaking horses. We only spent a few hours together on a boring flight." He winked at me before he hugged me to his rail-thin frame.

"Are you seeing her again?" I pressed.

"I'm here to celebrate with you," he countered, kissing my forehead.

"And I can mind my own business, right?"

He grinned. "Where's the rest of the brood?"

"They're all at Zara's house. Jonathan's practicing his godfather duties and Megan's meeting her baby cousin."

"Sounds good to me," Connor replied, taking my arm and leading me back to the office.

"Hey, the kitchen's that way," I protested, pointing over his shoulder.

"First things first. I want to see what you're doing

with Dad's office. You told me last week you were making changes."

I entered the room with its now-bare walls and empty coin cabinet. "I didn't throw anything out, at least not anything of value. I've set aside things for the three of you to divide up. I'm turning this into a playroom for my grandchildren."

"You've done a great job." He kissed my cheek, his curly red hair framing his gaunt features.

It had been years since Connor's hockey accident, and still he was so thin he worried me. But there was nothing I could do to change that today, or ever.

"It's great to have you home for the anniversary. Now, let's get dinner on the table for the starving horde."

"Mom, I'm so glad we're having this celebration, not only for you, but for Zara and Gregory."

"I'll miss them."

"Of course, but you'll enjoy visiting them in Atlanta."

"I will. Maybe we'll all have Christmas in Atlanta."

We'd just finished setting the dining room table when I saw Zara's car pull into the driveway. "They're here." I opened the front door, anxious to hold my family close.

As I reached to take Andrew's car seat from Gregory, we exchanged glances, and in that fraction of a second we both saw the other differently. I had come to really love and respect my son-in-law. Just in time to have him leave, darn it.

I ushered everyone into the house, then Zara, Jonathan and Connor held their usual hug-in. I gave them a few minutes to admire Andrew while I took Megan to the kitchen and set her up with a new box of Play Doh. Megan was unusually quiet. Jonathan hadn't said why Linda hadn't come with them, but it wasn't a good sign. "What color would you like today?" I asked Megan.

She hung her head; her lips formed a pout. "I don't want to play. I want my mommy."

My heart lurched at the sight of my granddaughter upset. Kneeling down beside her, I tucked a strand of her red-blond hair behind her ear. "Megan, honey, your mommy couldn't come. But you and I can have a good time together, right?"

"I don't want to. I want my mommy. My mommy's going away, and she's not coming back." Big shiny tears gathered on her lashes.

Was Linda leaving Jonathan? No, it couldn't have happened this quickly. Jonathan would've said something.

Did Megan think that her mother's leaving had anything to do with her? I held my granddaughter in my arms, and she rubbed the rings on my left hand. "My mommy cries and she says it's 'cause she's unhappy."

How did this child get caught up in all this? Why weren't Jonathan and Linda more careful about what they said in front of her? She was too young to understand what her parents were going through, and powerless to stop it. "Megan, I know you miss your mommy, but what about baby Andrew? Wouldn't you like to play with him?"

"I tried to. All he does is sleep." She began to cry in earnest.

Jonathan appeared at the door, frowning with concern. "Megan, what is it?"

"I want Mommy," she sobbed. She climbed into her father's arms and buried her face in his neck. He glanced at me with a look of pure misery as he stroked his daughter's hair.

"We need to talk," I whispered.

He nodded and started toward the living room with Megan in his arms, huddled against her father's chest. I could hear Connor and Gregory laughing together and fervently wished that Jonathan would again be able to laugh.

When he returned, he was alone. "Zara and Megan get along great. Zara's taking her up to see the dolls in the attic."

"So, what's going on with you and Linda? And what about her pregnancy?" I asked, fearing that what I'd just witnessed with my granddaughter meant Jonathan was about to get a divorce.

But his expression held hope. "We've decided to go back into counseling to see if we can work things out. Linda and I talked about the baby. She's not as depressed as she was, but I'm not sure what that means. Anyway, at least she's willing to talk."

"Jonathan, where did Megan get the idea that her mother's leaving?"

His face paled. "I don't know. We haven't said a word to her, not a word."

"Are you sure?" I saw the pain on Jonathan's face, and wished I could take back my words.

"Mom, I'm doing the best I can. When I get back, I'll talk to Linda and see how we can help Megan." He sat in the chair near the window, his eyes downcast. "Mom, what am I going to do? I don't want to lose Linda and my family. But I don't have any idea how to stop it."

"Do you still love her?"

His head came up, and a look of determination shone in his eyes. "I've loved her since the day I met her in American history class during our junior year."

"Have you told her that?"

He shoved his hands through his close-cropped hair, his jaw clenched. "No, Mom. I guess I haven't. Not for quite a while. I've been working so hard. She's been busy. There never seem to be enough hours in the day. Our next-door neighbors moved this spring...they were our best friends. Linda misses Elaine."

Listening to Jonathan took me back to the days when finding time for each other was almost impossible, and outside influences seemed to absorb all our energies. We let our lives bury our connection to each other to the point that we nearly divorced. It took love, understanding and the willingness to try again to save our marriage.

Sam's words about giving love a second chance chimed in my head.

"Jonathan, someone special in my life told me that

love should be given a second chance. Your father and I had that, and I'll be forever grateful. What I want you to understand is that love is worth every sacrifice. You love Linda. She's carrying your child. Go to her, and tell her how much she means to you."

His anxious gaze met mine; tears swam in his eyes. "Do you believe it's that simple?"

"I honestly don't know, but neither will you unless you try. Get on the phone and call Linda. Tell her you love her and you want her on the first available flight. Tell her we're all waiting for her, that you'll pick her up at the airport. Tell her Megan misses her. That we all do."

Relief and surprise chased each other across Jonathan's face. "You think it'll work?"

Even at this stage of my life, I figured I didn't know much about anything, but I could still wing it. "Any woman worth her salt won't be able to refuse your invitation. And I'll take care of Megan while you and Linda spend time alone together. Now, hurry!"

Without a backward glance, Jonathan strode out of the kitchen, up the stairs and into his old bedroom. I watched him go, my pulse thudding. I was still standing at the bottom of the staircase when Zara appeared at the top.

"What's Jonathan doing in his room?" Zara asked as she descended.

"Urgent telephone call that can only be made in his room."

"Having to do with Linda, I assume."

"You assume correctly."

"And you had a hand in it, I'm sure," Zara said, peering down at me.

"I did."

"Do you suppose the day will ever come when you *won't* have to rescue one or another of us?"

I hoped not, but I didn't say so. I didn't want the label of clingy mother, or worse, meddling mother-in-law. "Simply stating the facts."

"The way Dad would have?"

I nodded my head as I took in my beautiful daughter, standing there so straight. There'd been a change in her. She seemed much happier, more content.

"Want some help getting dinner on the table, Mom?" Zara asked.

"As a matter of fact, I do."

We linked arms and walked to the kitchen. "Where's Megan?"

"In my old room. I brought the dollhouse and furniture down from the attic and she's waist-deep in dolls and doll clothes. She's the sweetest little girl."

"Thanks for being so good to her. She's going through a rough patch right now with her parents talking divorce."

"Oh, Mom, I hope that doesn't happen. I can't imagine how Jonathan will cope if he's separated from Megan. He loves her so much. He's as involved with her as Linda is, although Linda will probably get custody if there's a divorce."

"I had no idea they were having problems until he told me the last time he was here."

"I didn't, either," Zara said as we entered the kitchen.

"Didn't what?" Connor asked, getting a beer out of the fridge.

"Jonathan and Linda."

"Oh, yeah. Where is he, by the way?"

"Upstairs calling Linda to see if she'll change her mind and join us," I answered.

Connor glanced from Zara to me. "He might need a little moral support," he said half to himself as he put his beer on the counter and walked toward the stairs.

Zara and I worked in companionable silence, making gravy and preparing a salad. Then we got the roast and baked potatoes out of the oven. I took a moment to check on Gregory and Andrew in the living room. Gregory was rocking Andrew.

As we stood at the counter putting the finishing touches on the meal, Zara turned to me. "Mom, are you really okay with our plans to move to Atlanta?"

"I'll miss you and Andrew and Gregory so much, and there'll be days I'll wish you could move back home. But I want whatever makes you happy, and your life with Gregory makes you very happy. I see that."

"And you? What makes you happy?"

"Having my family here today. Having Kate as my friend. Discovering that I want to help Phillip Bannister if I can. Feeling that I've come to terms with your father being gone. And of course keeping little Andrew while you go house hunting in Atlanta."

"And Sam?"

I could feel my cheeks flush. "He's become a special part of my life. Who knows what'll happen next?"

"But you're willing to take a chance on him?"

"I am."

"I haven't been very fair to you where Sam's concerned, and it was Gregory who showed me that I had to let you make your own choices, the same way you were letting me make mine." Zara stopped carving the roast and wrapped her arms around my neck, the way she once did with her father. "Mom, I'm pleased you and Sam are enjoying each other's company."

"I've been wondering how you felt about him," I said, sighing in relief.

"I'm okay with it, but it's also good to hear you say you're okay with our move. It means so much to me. I want you to enjoy yourself when I'm gone."

My darling daughter, you've got your wish. No matter what happens from here on, I will be happy for you, for Gregory, Baby Andrew, Connor, Jonathan, Linda and Megan and my as-yet-unborn grandchild.

I hugged her. "I will," I whispered, and meant it.

A SHORT WHILE LATER, after Megan had been put to bed and Jonathan announced that he had convinced Linda to come, we were all seated around the table sipping coffee and finishing off the chocolate cake when Jonathan came in with a small white box.

"What's that?" I asked.

"Call it an anniversary gift," Jonathan said, handing it to me.

I opened it. Nestled in purple satin was a miniature horse-drawn carriage. "Where did you get this?"

"In an antique store in Seattle. I thought it was the perfect gift for this occasion."

I smiled to myself. "Andrew would've gotten a good chuckle out of this."

"So what's with the gift?" Connor asked.

"Yeah, don't keep us in suspense," Zara chimed in from the other side of the table where she was nursing baby Andrew.

"It's about what happened to Mom and Dad on their wedding day," Jonathan said, his eyes locking on me, a smile lighting his face.

"How come you know about it and not us?" Zara inquired, exchanging glances with Connor.

"Because when Jonathan was little, he and I used to go through the photo albums for something to do. We had no extra money for movies, and we didn't have cable TV." I shrugged as Jonathan and I continued to smile at each other. "And he was tired of the books I had for him. So, I told him stories about my life growing up, including the story of my wedding day."

"They were all great, but the wedding one was my favorite," Jonathan added.

I got a thumbs-up from him.

Connor and Gregory pulled their chairs closer to the table. Zara put Andrew in the bassinet we'd recovered from the attic and brought the coffee pot to the table. "So, let's hear it."

I put the horse and carriage ornament on the table in front of me. "It was October twenty-third, 1967…"

Teetering on my white satin pumps, I clutch the train of my wedding dress against my thigh and hold my bridal bouquet of lily of the valley and white roses in the other hand, the one with my shiny gold wedding band.

Andrew's hand rests on the small of my back as he guides me to the waiting carriage and twin bay horses hired by my uncle Max.

I feel like Cinderella as I move down the stone walkway from the church to the carriage. I smile up at Andrew, relieved to have my new husband alone for a few moments.

"Allow me, Mrs. Martin," he says, holding open the half door of the carriage.

"Thank you, Mr. Martin," I say, my heart as light as a feather. I manage to seat myself on the soft gray velvet and pull my wedding gown over to let Andrew sit down.

"Smile at the cameras," he whispers in my ear.

Surrounded by the sweet scent of lilies and roses, I lean back and let happiness roll over me. Every little detail of the wedding had gone perfectly. Now we had only the reception at the Women's Institute hall to worry about, and then we'd be off on our honeymoon.

"Sorry for dropping the ring," Andrew says, looking truly contrite.

"It's okay. We were both nervous."

He gazes into my eyes, the sun glinting off his dark red hair while a smile raises the corners of his mouth. "I'll make it up to you tonight, Mrs. Martin. I promise."

"I'll keep you to that," I say, winking at him.

He kisses me over the snap of flashbulbs and the call for "more."

"Are we ready to go to the reception?" asks Barry Snow, Andrew's best man and the driver of our landau carriage.

"Ready."

"Then we're off." Barry gives us a jaunty salute as he reaches for the reins and snaps them gently.

The crack and crunch of carriage wheels on gravel, the elegant way the horses move in rhythm, makes me glad I accepted Uncle Max's offer to provide us with this horse-drawn carriage.

I snuggle into Andrew, delighting in the day and the dappled light through the arch of trees. We reach the end of the lane and begin to turn right onto the narrow country road when, out of the corner of my eye, I see Mrs. Barnaby's pet terrier leaping and bobbing across the field of clover straight toward the team of horses.

I love animals, all animals—except that yapping excuse for a dog. He's a biter and a barker, and he's headed straight for us. "Barry, look out!"

Too late. The dog runs into the path of the horses. They rear up in unison, their front legs flailing the air. Then their hooves hit the ground with a bone-jarring thud, and the horses speed down the road toward the ditch, with us bouncing along behind them in the carriage.

"Andrew!" I scream.

"Barry!" Andrew yells.

"Slow down, easy now," Barry calls out over the wind and the reins flying loose around him as he clings to the side of the carriage.

"Barry, stop them!" Andrew and I yell in unison as the carriage does a dip and dive through the rain-filled ditch, and up onto the other side with a rattling thump that tosses me up and over the seat.

"Emily!" Andrew grabs me around the waist to pull me back just as the horses swerve, throwing Barry onto the ground.

Within seconds Barry's a lump on the earth behind us as we gather speed and sail past a line of poplar trees. "Andrew, stop these horses!" I shout, my nails digging into the back of the front seat.

"I don't know how," he yells back, his words jerked from his lips like scraps of paper scattered to the wind.

I can see that we aren't far from the bank of the river…and I can't swim. The ground is rushing past us; my bouquet flies away and in that terrifying moment I realize that only one action can save us.

One of us has to rescue the reins.

I dive forward into the driver's seat. But the metal hoop of my wedding dress catches on the back and I land headfirst on the floor. My shoulders are jammed against the seat, my rear end is in the air, and the skirt hoop of my wedding dress fans out to show the whole world my behind.

"Andrew!" I scream at the top of my lungs, bracing my hands on the floor.

"Whoa, boys!" Andrew yells above the wind and the racket of hooves and jangling harness.

The horses come to an abrupt halt. Andrew slams over the back of the seat, landing on his knees on the floor beside me.

Our shock hangs like icicles over the sudden silence. Afraid that any move could send the horses on their merry way once more, we stare at each other upside down and wait anxiously.

"What are they doing?" I whisper as I wrestle my hands free of my skirt and try to turn myself upright in the narrow space.

"Who?" Andrew looks at me as if I'm speaking another language.

"The horses," I hiss at him.

He peeks over the front of the carriage. "They're looking back at us." Andrew tilts his head, bird-like. "Your nose is really cute from this angle," he says.

"My nose?" Thinking he's suffered a concussion, I peer at him from my upside-down position. "My *nose?*"

"Never mind." He reaches for me. "Here, let me help you."

"Forget about me. Get those reins in your hands and hold them. I don't want those two taking off again. They're headed for the river."

"Yeah, you're right." Cautiously Andrew works his fingers through the reins dangling over the front of the carriage.

I do a handstand that brings me back up on the seat, where I pull the hoop of my skirt into position. I arrange my wedding dress around me as carefully as I can—a difficult task in a seat meant for one scrawny driver. All this under the watchful eyes of a pair of skittish horses who seem to be waiting for some sort of signal from us.

"What do we do now?" Andrew asks softly, helping me arrange my floppy skirt and disheveled veil.

"Have you ever driven a team of horses?" I ask quietly.

"No, have you?"

"No. Any ideas?" I ask.

"Not at the moment."

Loath to let those two up front know just how desperate we are, I glance behind us and see Barry limping across the field toward the carriage.

"Maybe we don't have to worry. Hold those reins absolutely steady," I whisper. "I'll make a dash for reinforcements."

"No, I'll do it. You'll ruin your dress."

I look at the horses, the proximity of the river and back at Andrew. "Honey, I can't swim, and there's no place to tether the horses."

Gathering my skirts and forcing the badly bent hoop into an irregular oval shape, I ease myself out of the carriage and start back toward Barry. The breeze catches the edge of my bent hoop and I feel my feet begin to lift from under me...

Remembering that day as if it were yesterday, I leaned my elbows on the table and ran my fingers over the miniature horse and carriage. "Yeah, that was quite a ride. I'll never forget the look on your father's face when I told him I couldn't swim."

"Continue the story. Did you make it to the hall, and how did your reception go?" Connor asked, laughing gently.

"It went fine—once we managed to get the horses and the carriage out of the field and back on the road. Not trusting Uncle Max's mode of transport anymore, we got a ride to the reception with one of the guests. I had a bump on my temple as big as a goose egg, and I spent the next little while in the ladies' room with Sheila, my maid of honor, trying to comb my hair and fix my makeup."

"Was your dress all right?" Zara asked.

"It was a disaster since part of the hem was torn out when I caught my heel in it. Sheila had a set of nail scissors with her and we snipped the hoop out of my skirt."

"Tell them what happened next," Jonathan

prompted as he toyed with the ornament, a wide smile on his face.

"All the guests were staring at us when we got into the reception hall. I suppose they were wondering what went wrong after they saw us go flying down the road and across the fields. During the toast to the groom, Barry stood up in front of everyone with the knees torn out of his pants and his tie muddied, and wanted to know why Andrew hadn't learned to drive a team of horses."

"What did Dad say?" Zara asked.

"He said it didn't matter whether he could drive a team of horses or not. He wouldn't have missed that ride for the world. I can still see his smile when he leaned over and kissed me, pulling me up next to him. He said that racing over the fields with me at his side would be one of his fondest memories."

"And what did you say?" asked Connor.

I had a sudden flash of insight, or was it memory? It had been a slow, winding road, our marriage, with its share of ups and downs.

Those last days of Andrew's illness had destroyed any illusions I had about the fairness of life, leaving me unable to trust in the future. And now I was about to give up my daughter to a life I'd have no part in, and I might also lose my daughter-in-law to a web of marital discord.

Yet with my memories of Andrew to guide me, I held to the hope that there were better days ahead.

I returned to Connor's question. "What did I say?"

I glanced around the table: at Jonathan, my oldest son, at Zara, the daughter of my dreams, at Gregory, who made Zara so happy, and finally at Connor, the son whose bravery and courage after his hockey accident taught us all a lesson about life.

"I told your father and our wedding guests that I wouldn't change places with anyone."

"Oh, Mom, that's so sweet." Zara sighed. "I wish Dad was here for this."

"I do, too, but he's not, and that's what I wanted to say to all of you. This has been the hardest fifteen months of my life, and I would never have made it through without your love and support. But I'm ready to move forward. I'm not saying there won't be more bad moments. However, I'm going to find a life that will satisfy me. Your father's letters made it clear that he wants me to be happy."

The room was silent except for the ticking of Uncle Max's grandfather clock. Had I made a mistake? Maybe my children really *weren't* ready to hear me say those words.

"This is wonderful news," Zara said a few seconds later, and the boys chimed in.

AFTER THE DISHES WERE washed and put away, Jonathan entered the back porch where I was sitting alone with my thoughts, and sat down beside me.

In the muted light, I studied his face, the familiar planes and angles, a poignant reminder of Andrew. Yet as I looked at him, I could see that his face was different from his father's. His lips were fuller, his cheekbones a little more prominent. And when he turned toward me, it struck me that Jonathan's resemblance to his father was a genetic fact of life, but my son was his own person, and it was up to me to play down the resemblance and to see Jonathan as the man he was.

"That was a great dinner, Mom," he said.

"Yes, and it was so nice having everyone together before Zara has to move to Atlanta."

Connor had gone to Zara's place, since he had to fly out the next day and wanted to spend time with his nephew.

"I'm on my way to the airport to pick up Linda. Are you going to be all right by yourself?"

"More importantly, are *you* all right?"

He sat back in his chair. "Yeah, Mom. I'll be fine," he said, linking his hands behind his head and staring up at the ceiling.

Seeing my son twice in the past weeks had shown me how tired he was, how hard he worked. The fact that he and Linda had so little time for each other increased my concern about their future happiness.

"Jonathan, whatever happens in the next few days with Linda, I want you to take it slow. You both need the chance to reconnect and give each other your undivided attention."

"We will. And thanks for what you said earlier."

"What's that?"

"About telling her how much I love her. At first I

didn't think I could get the words out. Somehow, saying something like that made me feel vulnerable and afraid that if Linda didn't feel the same way, I'd be making a complete fool of myself."

Oh, how I remember the fear of making a fool of myself for love, especially the day the lawyer's papers arrived.

"Have you made a hotel reservation for you and Linda?"

"I did, Mom, but are you sure you want to do this? I've explained to Megan that I'm going to pick up Mommy at the airport. She wanted to wait up for her mother. I read to her until she fell asleep, but she might fuss when she wakes up and we aren't here."

"Hey, you're talking to a professional mom. I can handle it. Go on. Spend the night with your wife. Or a few days if you need more time. I'll look after Megan."

He rose, kissed me on the cheek and crossed the porch in two easy strides. "Thanks, Mom."

"You're more than welcome."

Standing in the door, I watched him pull out of the driveway into the street. It had been a perfect day with a nearly perfect ending, I mused to myself. All that was needed to make it complete was for Jonathan and Linda to find their way back to each other.

From across the lawn I heard Sam whistling. I hadn't talked to him since the night he told me he loved me. I wasn't sure how I felt or what to say, and Sam had been considerate enough not to press the issue. After the emotion of today, and the realization that in a few months I'd have no family living near me, I felt the need to connect with someone. "You can stop hiding in the bushes and have a glass of wine with me, if you like."

"Thought you'd never ask," he said, vaulting across the dug-up area where the hedge had been. "Did I tell you they're coming tomorrow to put in the new fence?"

"No, you didn't, but if you'll help me with the wine-glasses and the bottle, we can sit on the porch and you can tell me the whole story."

"Oh, I have a lifetime of stories to tell you."

We settled on the porch with a bottle of Merlot on the table between us, a magical night surrounded by neighborhood sounds: Bernie French playing his piano two houses away, a sprinkler wheezing next door and laughter emanating from across the street.

"Did you have a good dinner?" Sam asked, taking a sip of his wine.

"Yes. And I'm babysitting Megan for a day or two. Jonathan has gone to the airport to pick up Linda. She's arriving on a red-eye flight from Seattle."

"So this would have been your fortieth anniversary."

"Yeah, and we had a great time tonight. But it was sort of bittersweet, since this will probably be one of the last meals I'll have with Zara and Gregory for a while. They're moving to Atlanta."

"Oh, dear." Sam reached out and squeezed my hand. "Are you all right with that?"

"I have to be. It's her life." I glanced over, waiting for him to remove his hand from mine.

He didn't.

Instead he moved his chair closer. "Emily Martin, you don't always have to be strong. In fact, I'm willing and able to be strong for you."

His eyes connected with mine, and in the shadowed light of the porch, I saw such warmth and concern in them, I wanted to cry out. "Sometimes I wish I could wave a magic wand and make everything okay for my family," I said, all the pent-up worry over my children suddenly rushing forward.

"What's wrong, Emily?"

My heart twisted at the sight of this man sitting so close to me, a man willing to show he cared by listening to my concerns. "I can't let Zara know it, but I'm devastated at the thought of her leaving. I'm panicked by the possibility that Linda and Jonathan may get a divorce. I'm not sure I can cope alone."

"Emily, you're not alone. You haven't been since the day you moved in here. When I saw you that first day with your blond hair pulled up off your face, the look of excitement in your blue eyes as you strolled around the property, I had to admit I experienced a serious infatuation."

"Sam, I wish I could tell you I—"

"Don't. You don't have to say anything. Just listen. I've waited years for you. And I'll wait years more if I have to."

Overwhelmed by his words and the love I saw in

his eyes, I leaned closer and kissed him. But what started out as a kiss of appreciation changed instantly as he took my head in his hands, angling my lips to his. With a groan, he pulled me to my feet and held me against him.

Clinging to him, I pressed my body to his, savoring the moment. He kissed my lips, my face, running his fingers over my back...

"Sam," I gasped, my body quivering in anticipation. "We can't do this. I have a child asleep upstairs, and Connor's coming home...."

Slowly he smoothed the hair from my face, his breathing erratic, his eyes dark. "Emily, I want you, but not unless the time is right."

"I want you. I do," I said, pressing my body to his.

Sam leaned his head back, his chest heaving under my fingers. "I've waited too long to settle for casual sex. For me, making love is just that—making love to someone I care about, someone who cares about me. Are you all right with that?"

"Of course." Not knowing what else to say, I sat back down in the chair and waited for my pulse to slow.

Silence filled the space between us, and somehow the night seemed less magical.

Sam left shortly after that, and I went into the house to wait for Connor to return from Zara's. I rattled around my empty house, putting the place mats back in the drawer, feeding Fergus and making myself a solitary cup of tea.

TWO DAYS LATER, AFTER I'd driven Connor to the airport and dropped Megan off at Zara's, I arrived back home to find workmen putting the finishing touches on the new wrought-iron fence.

"What do you think, Mrs. Martin?" asked Darnell Sparks, a young man who'd been a student of mine, as he closed the tailgate of his Ford half ton. He'd had only passing interest in history and geography, but he was a whiz at anything mathematical.

"Lovely," I announced, searching Sam's property for some sign of him.

As the truck pulled away from the curb, I heard Sam whistling tunelessly somewhere near the back of his house. After the other night I wasn't sure how to behave around him. I wanted to see him again, of that much I was certain, but after that… I fiddled with the branches of a wisteria as I waited to see if he'd come over.

I didn't have long to wait.

"What do you say we celebrate?" he asked, coming across the lawn and around the new fence with a bottle of champagne and two tapered flutes in his hands.

I had to acknowledge, at least to myself, that the sight of Sam walking toward me made my day. "A celebration is definitely in order."

I followed him up the steps to the back porch and put my purse down beside what had become my wicker chair while Sam tucked his long body into his.

With the skill of a barman, he popped the cork on

the champagne and poured. "Here you are," he said, his voice filled with pleasure.

"A toast," I said. "To our new fence."

"And to good times ahead for both of us."

"Do you believe that?"

"I do. You and I have become friends, and we've got lots of opportunities to explore the possibility of more. In the meantime, we can simply enjoy each other's company."

What else could I offer this man who was so kind to me, who said he loved me and had for some time? "You probably already know this, but I felt very lucky in my marriage to Andrew."

He nodded.

"Anyway, as of now, I'm feeling lucky again."

"Do I have that effect on you?" he asked, hope shining in his eyes.

"Yes, you do. You make me feel that my life is destined to be pretty special."

"Starting with the fence?"

"Starting with the fact that in my experience few men ever make such a beautiful confession of love as you did the other night—especially without expecting something in return."

"I'm not through with you yet," he said, waggling his eyebrows, Groucho Marx style.

I laughed…. I seemed to be doing a lot of that lately.

"Speaking of confessions, I have another one I want to make."

"I'm all ears," I teased, taking a sip of champagne.

He twirled the stem of his glass between his fingers and leaned forward. "I didn't tell you this, because I didn't want to upset you. But someone else was involved in the fence project."

I stared at him. "Someone else?"

"Yeah. There's one conversation I had with Andrew that I've never told a soul about. It was a week before he went into the hospital for the last time. He and I were sitting out here, talking about his need to feel that you'd be able to move on. In that uncluttered way he had, he confronted me with the fact that he knew I was in love with you. I tried to deny it, but he saw right through me. He said he wanted his wife and his best friend to be happy, and if he could do anything at all to help things along, he would."

My throat tightened, and I stared at him. "Help things along?"

He nodded. "Andrew was the one who came up with the idea of a fence. He said you couldn't be won over with showy presents or fancy dinners, but you loved your gardens. He decided that making plans for something related to our adjoining gardens was the perfect way for us to get together.

"I thought he was nuts, but I didn't say so. I did remind myself that no one knew you better than he did. So I waited, hoping for an opportunity to bring up the subject. Little Andrew's arrival seemed like the right time to take a chance." He sighed deeply and took a gulp of his champagne, then glanced over at me, a wry expression on his face. "The dance lessons were my backup plan."

I was about to open my mouth when Jonathan and Linda arrived.

They got out of the car and walked up the path, Jonathan's arm around Linda. "Hi, Mom. Hi, Sam," Linda said, a huge smile on her face as she entered the porch. "How'd you manage with Megan the last couple of days?" she asked, tucking her fingers into Jonathan's hand.

"Just fine. I dropped her off at Zara's on the way back from taking Connor to the airport."

I wanted to ask about their relationship, but decided to see what they had to say. But of course with Sam here, they might feel reluctant to talk.

Obviously sensitive about the situation, Sam stood up, preparing to leave. "Nice to see both of you, but I should get going."

"Beautiful fence," Jonathan said. "A joint project of the Bannister and Martin families?"

"Yes, Sam made all the arrangements. Isn't it gorgeous?" I interjected, wanting to be sure Sam got credit for the job.

"And doesn't it add a pleasant touch to the grounds," Linda murmured, still holding her husband's hand as she gazed lovingly into his face.

They were acting like two people in love. I could jump up and down with happiness.

"Why don't the four of us celebrate the installation of the new fence," Jonathan said. "Dinner's on me."

"Oh, no. You need to enjoy being together as a family. Plus I should tidy up around the new posts, put the tools away, that sort of stuff," Sam said.

"Sam, I haven't had an opportunity to say this before, but I want to thank you for mowing the lawn and helping my mother when you could. Living so far from home, I'm glad I can rely on you."

Sam beamed. "You're welcome."

"So, as part of my thank-you, I'd like you to join us for dinner."

Sam glanced at me. I nodded, happy to be going out with my family and my friend.

"I'd love to go with you," Sam said, holding his arm out to me. "Where to?"

"Someplace that serves champagne, obviously," Jonathan said, gesturing to the two champagne flutes and winking at Sam.

EPILOGUE

"HURRY!" I YELLED at the taxi driver as I braced myself for the I-5 turnoff to Meridian Street in Bellingham, Washington. "I don't want to miss *this* arrival," I muttered to myself.

"The hospital's a few blocks away. I can't go much faster, but if you're sick, we could stop at a clinic."

"I'm late for my grandchild's birth…again."

All my plans had been trashed when the flight from New York to Seattle was delayed. When I landed at Bellingham International Airport, Jonathan called me on my cell to say that Linda was in the delivery room. He was excited to be her labor coach; they'd spent hours in class, and were looking forward to bringing their son into the world. They'd decided to name him Connor Andrew Martin.

I wanted to be there when they got out of the delivery room. I tried to stay calm as the taxi made its way toward St. Joseph Hospital. "How much farther?"

"A couple of blocks." The driver slammed on the brakes as a pedestrian stepped off the curb.

"What next?" I mumbled, clutching my purse to my

chest as the air freshener dangling from the rearview mirror swung wildly.

I grabbed the door handle and did my best to relax in the lumpy seat. There was nothing I could do but wait.

The past seven months had been better than I could ever have imagined. Zara was happily settled in Atlanta with Gregory and Andrew. And of course Andrew was growing so fast I couldn't believe my eyes. So far I'd been to visit their new home once and they'd come to my house for a few days at Christmas, but mostly I relied on a new computer program called Skype, which allowed me to see Zara, Gregory and little Andrew every day. Before she moved to Atlanta, Zara had arranged for an assessment of Phillip, resulting in an improvement of his reading…with a little help from me.

Connor and I had a fabulous trip to Chile, but I was never so glad to get home in my life—because of Sam.

I missed him so much I nearly left early. But of course I couldn't do that, since it would've hurt Connor's feelings. So I settled for calling him every other night. We'd become very close these past few months, and we shared so many interests other than gardening—our love for our families, reading—and Sam was the best cook on the planet.

But most of all I'd grown to love him, and last Sunday, he'd proposed to me. I hadn't given him my answer yet, because I wasn't sure if marriage was right for me at this point in my life.

After all, Sam and I had our own lives, and we had the luxury of being next door to each other. We were both independent and liked our own space. And where would we live if we got married? I couldn't leave my house.

There were so many things to consider.

Sam, being Sam, just smiled his enigmatic smile when I said I hadn't decided about marriage.

And of course when the call came from Jonathan, I packed my bags and headed out the door.

As he drove me to the airport, Sam said he was planning a surprise for me. With Sam, you never quite knew what to expect. All those years I'd believed he was simply an eccentric professor, but I'd also discovered that his eccentricities were among his best traits.

Who would've thought there could be so many changes in my life in so short a time? And all of them positive.

"Here we are, ma'am. St. Joseph Hospital main entrance."

I passed him the fare plus tip, then followed him to the back of his car, where he extracted my suitcase.

I shouldered my purse and moved quickly toward the doors, the hurried thump and clack of my suitcase wheels accompanying me. And wouldn't you know? Another one of those dreaded revolving doors!

But nothing could deter me. I swept into the hospital, my suitcase at my heels and went straight to the elevator. Jonathan had given me instructions on how to find their room. Once on the maternity floor, I scanned the various signs as I checked my notes.

"Mom!"

I turned and there walking right behind me, was my son, his face beaming. "He's here, and Linda's fine."

He broke into a run, his arms out, drawing me into a bear hug that swept the air from my lungs. "He's beautiful. Seven pounds, four ounces. Linda was great, and I'm so proud of her."

"Your good coaching made a difference, I'm sure."

"It did, and I wished I'd taken the coaching course when Megan was born. I wouldn't have missed a moment of it. There aren't many things as beautiful as being with your wife when your child is born," Jonathan said, his tone muffled by tears as his arms tightened around me.

Standing together like this, holding my son in my arms, I was reminded of another day not so long ago when I'd held him, fearing that his marriage to Linda might be over.

We all had so much to be thankful for.

Jonathan let me go, looking straight into my eyes, with an unmistakable expression of joy on his face. "I'm beyond happy."

He took my suitcase and we walked toward Linda's room. Seeing Jonathan's delight at being a father again, I was suddenly aware of how much Andrew would have enjoyed this.

"Dad would've been happy, too, wouldn't he Mom?" It was as if Jonathan had read my mind.

"He would've loved seeing his new grandson." The thought was sweet, the pain of loss now softened to a feeling of exquisite tenderness.

Jonathan stopped outside Linda's room and put his arm around my shoulder. "You still miss him."

"Always. But it's easier now."

"And Sam's part of why it's easier, isn't he?"

"He is."

"I'm glad for both of you."

"Me, too," I whispered.

With his arm still on my shoulder, Jonathan asked, "Are you ready to meet your new grandson?"

I smiled up into his eyes, my heart bursting with joy at being here with the son I've loved for over thirty-five years. "I can't wait to see your baby boy."

As he opened the door, I saw Linda sitting in the bed, her son cradled in her arms, her face shining with an inner glow.

She smiled at me, tears flowing unfettered down her cheeks. "He is so perfect."

I moved toward the bed, then remembered the hand-washing policy of the hospital and took a short detour to the sink. Ready for the moment I'd been waiting for all these months, I took baby Connor in my arms.

A sense of union as unfathomable as it was impossible to describe seemed to flow between us. I stared down into his tiny face, wanting to feel this way forever.

The baby pursed his tiny lips and squinted in my general direction. I smiled at him, raised his body to my face and held his cheek to mine, drawing his baby scent deep into my lungs.

"You're right. He's absolutely perfect," I murmured, glancing at Linda, my gaze connecting with hers. As her eyes left mine and moved to her son, I saw the naked love in her eyes.

"Would you like to hold him a little longer?" Linda asked.

I would have, but I remembered those early moments with my own babies, holding them in my arms, how precious they were. "I believe he needs his mom," I said.

"Yes, oh yes," she said, eagerly reaching for him. She took him from me, kissing his forehead as she cuddled him.

"Is Megan here?" I asked, wanting to see my granddaughter and hear her version of today. I was sure there'd be one—a child's point of view was always so delightful.

"My friend Elaine is bringing her over in a little while. I can't wait for her to see her little brother," she said as she held Connor.

A sudden bleat and tiny fists appeared pressed to his cheeks. "Look at that," I said, seeing his face grow pink as a frown took shape on his tiny forehead.

"Oh, Jonathan." I looked at my son as he moved to stand next to the bed, a small frown on his own face. "I remember when you did that. Your father and I used to chuckle at how you'd press your fists to your cheeks and howl. We thought it was so cute," I said, over the wails of my grandson.

Watching the way Jonathan and Linda moved to comfort their son, I realized that staying here right now would be an intrusion. Tiptoeing out of the room, I went down the corridor to the waiting room to call Sam.

I needed to tell him I got here safely, and that everything was fine. He answered on the first ring.

"You're not going to believe this," I told him, "but Jonathan's little boy looks and acts just like Jonathan."

"That makes sense, doesn't it?"

"Stop kidding with me. I'm serious. He's gorgeous."

"How are you doing?"

"I'm excited…and a little tired."

"And lonely perhaps?"

"More than perhaps. I miss you, Sam. You should've come with me to see this little boy and to experience a room full of happiness. Megan will be here any minute. Oh, Sam, why don't you change your mind and fly out here? Bellingham is a lovely place and we could have a mini-vacation together."

"You think so?" Sam said, his voice on the phone echoing in the room.

"There must be something wrong with the connection. I'm hearing an echo," I said.

"No echo. Turn around."

Sam? Here? It wasn't possible! "Where are you?" I asked, searching the waiting room.

"Remember the surprise I promised?" Sam said, coming toward me from the corridor by the vending machines.

"*You're* the surprise?"

"Do you like it?" he asked, then kissed me thoroughly.

"I love it but you could've warned me."

He leaned back, grinning in that way of his. "And spoil the surprise? You've got to be kidding."

"We should tell Jonathan and Linda that they have another guest."

"No need to. We're not staying. I've booked us on a flight to Honolulu."

"Honolulu?"

Raising one eyebrow, he nodded. "With Jonathan's encouragement."

Stalling for time while I thought about it, I said, "What about Fergus? And Bouncer?" I'd actually gotten to like his dog.

"Taken care of, so stop looking for excuses."

"I'm not."

"You are, but here's the plan. We'll visit overnight with your family, then we're going to Seattle and taking a morning flight to Hawaii. We'll visit Jonathan and Linda again on the way back. After that, we're going home and getting married. I've decided I can't wait any longer. Any questions?"

I looked at this man who'd taken such a role in my life seven months ago and made me feel happier than I'd ever dreamed possible. He understood when I had sad moments over losing Andrew, he understood how much I loved my family and supported me in every way he could.

Now he wanted to marry me…. "Sam Bannister, I accept your proposal of marriage."

"That's the right answer," he said, his arms encircling me again.

"When is the ceremony? Should I buy something?"

"You can buy a whole new wardrobe in Honolulu. Although I wouldn't get my hopes up if I were you."

"About what?"

"About wearing very much of it for long." He kissed me again, only this time I heard clapping.

"Way to go, Sam," Jonathan said.

I unlocked my lips from Sam's and turned to my son. "You knew?"

"Yes, of course. And I approve. So do Zara and Connor."

I allowed my gaze to linger on Jonathan before glancing at Sam. "What's a girl to do?"

"Exactly."

Hours later as the cab drove us to a lovely little B and B that Sam had booked for the night, I decided to come right out with it. "Sam, I don't think we should wait to get married. I mean, life's too short."

"Whoa! What brought this on?"

"Something you said about second chances. I don't want this one to slip away."

"It won't. I promise." He drew me close to him, his lips brushing my cheek. I breathed in his scent, the warmth of his skin on mine, and knew in my heart that this was exactly what Andrew wanted.

Live life to the fullest.

* * * * *

Eight years ago Matt Shaffer had vanished out of Natalie Rothchild's life, leaving behind a one-line note tucked under a pillow that had grown cold: *I'm sorry, but this just isn't going to work.*

That was it. No explanation, no real indication of remorse. The note had been as clinical and compassionless as an eviction notice, which, in effect, it had been, Natalie thought as she navigated through the morning traffic. Matt had written the note to evict her from his life.

She'd spent the next two weeks crying, breaking down without warning as she walked down the street, or as she sat staring at a meal she couldn't bring herself to eat.

Candace, she remembered with a bittersweet pang,

had tried to get her to go clubbing in order to get her to forget about Matt.

She'd turned her twin down, but she did get her act together. If Matt didn't think enough of their relationship to try to contact her, to try to make her understand why he'd changed so radically from lover to stranger, then to hell with him. He was dead to her, she resolved. And he'd remained that way.

Until twenty minutes ago.

The adrenaline in her veins kept mounting.

Natalie focused on her driving. Vegas in the daylight wasn't nearly as alluring, as magical and glitzy as it was after dark. Like an aging woman best seen in soft lighting, Vegas's imperfections were all visible in the daylight. Natalie supposed that was why people like her sister didn't like to get up until noon. They lived for the night.

Except that Candace could no longer do that.

The thought brought a fresh, sharp ache with it.

"Damn it, Candy, what a waste," Natalie murmured under her breath.

She pulled up before the Janus casino. One of the three valets currently on duty came to life and made a beeline for her vehicle.

"Welcome to the Janus," the young attendant said cheerfully as he opened her door with a flourish.

"We'll see," she replied solemnly.

As he pulled away with her car, Natalie looked up at the casino's logo. Janus was the Roman god with two faces, one pointed toward the past, the other facing the future. It struck her as rather ironic, given what she was doing here, seeking out someone from her past in order to get answers so that the future could be settled.

The moment she entered the casino, the Vegas phenomena took hold. It was like stepping into a world where time did not matter or even make an appearance. There was only a sense of "now."

Because in Natalie's experience she'd discovered that bartenders knew the inner workings of any establishment they worked for better than anyone else, she made her way to the first bar she saw within the casino.

The bartender in attendance was a gregarious man in his early forties. He had a quick, sexy smile, which was probably one of the main reasons he'd been hired. His name tag identified him as Kevin.

Moving to her end of the bar, Kevin asked, "What'll it be, pretty lady?"

"Information." She saw a dubious look cross his brow. To counter that, she took out her badge. Granted she wasn't here in an official capacity, but Kevin didn't need to know that. "Were you on duty last night?"

Kevin began to wipe the gleaming black surface of the bar. "You mean during the gala?"

"Yes."

The smile gracing his lips was a satisfied one. Last night had obviously been profitable for him, she judged. "I caught an extra shift."

She took out Candace's photograph and carefully

placed it on the bar. "Did you happen to see this woman there?"

The bartender glanced at the picture. Mild interest turned to recognition. "You mean Candace Rothchild? Yeah, she was here, loud and brassy as always. But not for long," he added, looking rather disappointed. There was always a circus when Candace was around, Natalie thought. "She and the boss had at it and then he had our head of security escort her out."

She latched onto the first part of his statement. "They argued? About what?"

He shook his head. "Couldn't tell you. Too far away for anything but body language," he confessed.

"And the head of security?" she asked.

"He got her to leave."

She leaned in over the bar. "Tell me about him."

"Don't know much," the bartender admitted. "Just that his name's Matt Shaffer. Boss flew him in from L.A., where he was head of security for Montgomery Enterprises."

There was no avoiding it, she thought darkly. She was going to have to talk to Matt. The thought left her cold. "Do you know where I can find him right now?"

Kevin glanced at his watch. "He should be in his office. On the second floor, toward the rear." He gave her the numbers of the rooms where the monitors that kept watch over the casino guests as they tried their luck against the house were located.

Taking out a twenty, she placed it on the bar. "Thanks for your help."

Kevin slipped the bill into his vest pocket. "Anytime, lovely lady," he called after her. "Anytime."

She debated going up the stairs, then decided on the elevator. The car that took her up to the second floor was empty. Natalie stepped out of the elevator, looked around to get her bearings and then walked toward the rear of the floor.

"Into the Valley of Death rode the six hundred," she silently recited, digging deep for a line from a poem by Tennyson. Wrapping her hand around a brass handle, she opened one of the glass doors and walked in.

The woman whose desk was closest to the door looked up. "You can't come in here. This is a restricted area."

Natalie already had her ID in her hand and held it up. "I'm looking for Matt Shaffer," she told the woman.

God, even saying his name made her mouth go dry. She was supposed to be over him, to have moved on with her life. What happened?

The woman began to answer her. "He's—"

"Right here."

The deep voice came from behind her. Natalie felt every single nerve ending go on tactical alert at the same moment that all the hairs at the back of her neck stood up. Eight years had passed, but she would have recognized his voice anywhere.

* * * * *

*Why did Matt Shaffer leave heiress-turned-cop
Natalie Rothchild?
What does he know about the death of Natalie's
twin sister?
Come and meet these two reunited lovers and learn
the secrets of the Rothchild family in
THE HEIRESS'S 2-WEEK AFFAIR
by USA TODAY bestselling author
Marie Ferrarella.
The first book in Silhouette® Romantic Suspense's
wildly romantic new continuity,
LOVE IN 60 SECONDS!
Available April 2009.*

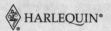

REQUEST YOUR FREE BOOKS!

2 FREE NOVELS PLUS 2 FREE GIFTS!

HARLEQUIN®

Super Romance®

Exciting, emotional, unexpected!

YES! Please send me 2 FREE Harlequin® Superromance® novels and my 2 FREE gifts (gifts are worth about $10). After receiving them, if I don't wish to receive any more books, I can return the shipping statement marked "cancel." If I don't cancel, I will receive 6 brand-new novels every month and be billed just $4.69 per book in the U.S. or $5.24 per book in Canada. That's a savings of close to 15% off the cover price! It's quite a bargain! Shipping and handling is just 25¢ per book*. I understand that accepting the 2 free books and gifts places me under no obligation to buy anything. I can always return a shipment and cancel at any time. Even if I never buy another book from Harlequin, the two free books and gifts are mine to keep forever.

135 HDN EEX7   336 HDN EEYK

Name	(PLEASE PRINT)
Address	Apt. #
City	State/Prov.	Zip/Postal Code

Signature (if under 18, a parent or guardian must sign)

Mail to the **Harlequin Reader Service:**
IN U.S.A.: P.O. Box 1867, Buffalo, NY 14240-1867
IN CANADA: P.O. Box 609, Fort Erie, Ontario L2A 5X3

Not valid to current subscribers of Harlequin Superromance books.

**Are you a current subscriber of Harlequin Superromance books
and want to receive the larger-print edition?
Call 1-800-873-8635 today!**

* Terms and prices subject to change without notice. Prices do not include applicable taxes. Sales tax applicable in N.Y. Canadian residents will be charged applicable provincial taxes and GST. Offer not valid in Quebec. This offer is limited to one order per household. All orders subject to approval. Credit or debit balances in a customer's account(s) may be offset by any other outstanding balance owed by or to the customer. Please allow 4 to 6 weeks for delivery. Offer available while quantities last.

Your Privacy: Harlequin is committed to protecting your privacy. Our Privacy Policy is available online at www.eHarlequin.com or upon request from the Reader Service. From time to time we make our lists of customers available to reputable third parties who may have a product or service of interest to you. If you would prefer we not share your name and address, please check here. ☐

HSR09

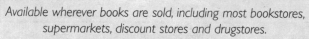

THE RAKE'S INHERITED COURTESAN
Ann Lethbridge

Christopher Evernden has been
assigned the unfortunate task of minding
Parisian courtesan Sylvia Boisette.
When Syliva sets off to find her father,
Christopher has no choice but to follow
and finds her kidnapped by an Irishman.
Once rescued, they finally succumb to
the temptation that has been brewing
between them. But can they see past the
limitations such a love can bring?

Available April 2009
wherever books are sold.

The Inside Romance newsletter has a NEW look for the new year!

Same great content, brand-new look!

The Inside Romance newsletter is a FREE quarterly newsletter highlighting our upcoming series releases and promotions!

Click on the Inside Romance link on the front page of **www.eHarlequin.com** or e-mail us at insideromance@harlequin.ca to sign up to receive your FREE newsletter today!

You can also subscribe by writing to us at: HARLEQUIN BOOKS Attention: Customer Service Department P.O. Box 9057, Buffalo, NY 14269-9057

Please allow 4-6 weeks for delivery of the first issue by mail.

COMING NEXT MONTH

Available April 14, 2009

#1554 HOME AT LAST • Margaret Watson
The McInnes Triplets
Fiona McInnes finally has the life in the Big Apple she'd always wanted. But when her father dies, she's forced to return home to help settle his estate. Now nothing's going as planned—including falling back in love with the man whose heart she shattered.

#1555 A LETTER FOR ANNIE • Laura Abbot
Going Back
Kyle Becker is over any feelings he had for Annie Greer. Then she returns to town, and suddenly he's experiencing those emotions again. But before he and Annie can share a future, Kyle must keep a promise to deliver a letter that could make her leave.

#1556 A NOT-SO-PERFECT PAST • Beth Andrews
Ex-con Dillon Ward has no illusions about who he is. Neither does his alluring landlord. But Nina Carlson needs him to repair her wrecked bakery—like, *yesterday*. And if there's one thing this struggling single mom knows, it's that nobody's perfect....

#1557 THE MISTAKE SHE MADE • Linda Style
Tori Amhearst can't keep her identity secret much longer. Ever since she brought Lincoln Crusoe home after an accident took away his memory, she's loved him on borrowed time. Because once Linc knows who she really is, she'll lose him forever.

#1558 SOMEONE LIKE HER • Janice Kay Johnson
Adrian Rutledge comes to Middleton expecting to find his estranged mother. He doesn't expect to find Lucy Peterson or a community that feels like home. Yet he gets this and more. Could it be that Lucy—and this town—is the family he's dreamed of?

#1559 THE HOUSE OF SECRETS • Elizabeth Blackwell
Everlasting Love
As soon as Alissa Franklin sees the old house, she knows it will be hers. With the help of handyman Danny—who has secrets of his own—she uncovers the truth about the original owners. But can a hundred-year-old romance inspire her to take a chance on love today?

HSRCNMBPA0309